DEAR MRS. RYAN, YOU'RE RUINING MY LIFE

DEAR MRS. RYAN, YOU'RE RUINING MY LIFE

JENNIFER B. JONES

WALKER & COMPANY

NEW YORK

Copyright © 2000 by Jennifer B. Jones

All the characters and events portrayed
in this work are fictitious.

First published in the United States of America in 2000
by Walker Publishing Company, Inc; first paperback
edition published in 2002.

Published simultaneously in Canada
by Fitzhenry and Whiteside,
Markham, Ontario L3R 4T8

Library of Congress Cataloging-in-Publication Data
Jones, Jennifer B.
    Dear Mrs. Ryan, you're ruining my life / Jennifer B.
Jones.
        p. cm.
    Summary: In an effort to get his mother to stop
writing about him in her books, fifth-grader Harvey
and his best friend decide to try to make a romantic
connection between her and their school principal.
    ISBN 0-8027-8728-2 (HC)
    [1. Mothers and sons—Fiction.   2. School stories.
3. Authors—Fiction.   4. Divorce—Fiction.
5. Friendship—Fiction.   6. Baseball—Fiction.]
I. Title.
    PZ7.J7203 De 2000
    [Fic]—dc21   99-054826
    ISBN 0-8027-7653-1 (paperback)

BOOK DESIGN BY JENNIFER ANN DADDIO

Printed in the United States of America
2 4 6 8 10 9 7 5 3 1

For my parents,
Menzo and Anne Brown,
who made the world of books
a real and wonderful part of my life.

CONTENTS

DEAR MRS. RYAN, YOU'RE RUINING MY LIFE

ONE

THE BEGINNING

I knew what was coming, and I tried to avoid it. When Mom opened my bedroom door to wake me up, I groaned, grabbed my stomach, and rolled around on my bed.

"My stomach is killing me," I said between moans. "I think I ate too much last night. Or maybe I'm coming down with the flu."

"Forget it, Harvey," Mom said. "Hustle up. Get out of bed."

"You're going to be embarrassed when I barf in front of the whole class and they have to send me home."

Mom laughed. "You tried this trick in third grade *and* in fourth grade. What made you think it would work this year?" She snapped on my ceiling light and backed out of the room.

"Mom!" I called.

"Out of bed, Harv," she answered from down the hall.

I dragged myself out of bed. What *had* I been think-ing? Mom could tell when I was sick and when I was faking. It was no use trying to trick her. But why did my teachers have to invite her in to talk to my class every year? Just because she writes books for kids my age. And just because kids my age love to read them. You'd think she was a celebrity or something. Nobody else's mother comes in every year. Nobody else's mom shares so much of their kid's personal life with the whole world.

"Harvey," Mom hollered up the stairs.

"Coming," I muttered. I shoved my legs into the jeans I'd worn to school the day before and grabbed a Yankees T-shirt from the pile of clean clothes by my door.

We were at my school less than an hour later. All visitors have to sign in at our main office, so of course that's where Mom and I went. Mom is friends with the secretary, so they started to chat. Mr. Stevens, our principal, must have heard them. He came out of his office, all smiles, and offered to escort us to the classroom.

"That's okay," I said. "I know where we're going."

"Harvey!" Mom said, then giggled like she does when she's nervous.

Mr. Stevens laughed. "Actually," he said, "I wanted to ask your mom if we could set up a couple more classroom visits. Mind if I walk with you?"

"That would be fine," Mom said.

No way was I going to walk to my classroom with my mom *and* my principal. "Uh, you guys take your time. I'll go on ahead. I have to be in my seat by the time the bell rings, right, Mr. Stevens?" I paused to grin. "Come in whenever, Mom. No hurry, really." And I was gone before they could answer.

Coming out of the office I almost plowed into my best friend, Seal Spicer.

"So you're here, Harv. I told you you wouldn't be able to fool your mom," she said.

I grabbed her elbow and steered her toward the stairs leading to our classroom on the second floor just as Mr. Stevens opened the office door and walked out with Mom.

Seal glanced over her shoulder as I sped her away. "Cute couple," she whispered in my ear.

We easily made it to our seats before the bell rang.

Mom slipped quietly into our room during morning announcements.

"Harvey, would you like to introduce your mother to us?" Mrs. Perkins asked after we said the pledge.

Not really, I wanted to say. We'd been working on character education all year, so it was only natural that an honest response popped into my head. But I've learned there are times when honesty is not the best policy. If adults want kids to be honest, they need to be careful what they ask.

"I think everybody knows my mom," I said politely.

"I haven't had the pleasure of meeting her," Mrs. Perkins said. Mrs. Perkins was new in town and finishing the school year for my regular fifth-grade teacher, who had moved away when her husband was transferred.

"Sorry," I mumbled and stood up by my desk. "Mom,

this is Mrs. Perkins. Mrs. Perkins, everybody, this is my mom, Leslie Ryan, the author of *The Skunk Who Came for Dinner* and all that other stuff."

"Well, Harvey," Mom said, grinning, "you don't have to sound so pleased."

Everybody laughed. I smiled and bobbed my head around, pretending to be amused.

"Harvey is right. All of you have probably heard me speak at least once. Instead of speaking to you today, I thought we'd try something a little different."

Different? I thought. Uh-oh. What's she going to throw at me now?

"Today," she was saying, "I'd like you to talk to me. Tell me what it is you like about the books you read."

Nobody said anything for almost a full minute. I guess they were surprised Mom wasn't there to entertain them. She wanted them to do some thinking. Mrs. Perkins started to look embarrassed as the time stretched on, but not Mom.

"What book are you all reading as a class right now?" she finally asked.

"*Skinnybones*!" everyone shouted all together.

"Wow!" Mom took a step backward as if they'd surprised her. "It sounds as if you like it. Why?"

And answers flew from all directions. "It's funny. It's about baseball. It's *short*." Mom laughed at that last one.

"When did you first know you were going to like *Skinnybones*?"

Some people said, "On the first page." Others said, "Right at the beginning." Without meaning to I blurted out, "Right from the very first sentence." I looked around quickly, but no one was paying attention to me.

"Yes." Mom nodded. "That's why the beginning is the most important part of a book."

Then she asked more questions about the books the kids were reading on their own. And except for Bethany not wanting to shut up about a book she was reading about the royal family, things went well. I looked at the clock and realized Mom would have to leave in a few minutes so we could go to our morning special. I was home safe.

Then I heard Mrs. Perkins say, "Perhaps Mrs. Ryan would answer a few questions before she leaves."

Mom nodded, and several hands shot in the air.

The first couple questions were, "How long does it take you to write a book?" and "How much money do you get?"

Stuff everybody wants to know, right? And her answer to both was, "It varies."

Please go home now, Mom.

But Mom called on Bethany. "Where do you get your ideas?" Bethany asked.

"My best ideas come from real life, from things that happen to me, or to people close to me."

I couldn't believe she said it. But she did it every time. See, the main characters in all Mom's books are always boys my age. It only takes a bear with very little brains to figure out which people close to her give her the best ideas. I could feel the kids turning to look at me.

Bethany was grinning as if she'd just sold a best-seller herself. "Do you ever put things that Harvey has done in your books?"

There it was, the question I'd been dreading. Everybody already knew the answer, but they had to ask anyway. I felt my face getting warm, and I hoped I wouldn't barf and make everything worse.

Seal tried to rescue me. "Come on, guys. Harvey's life isn't that interesting."

Everyone laughed. I looked at Seal. Our eyes connected, and I gave her a grateful nod.

But Bethany wasn't through yet. She was waving her whole arm around and didn't wait to be called on before blabbing out, "But Mrs. Ryan, didn't Harvey catch an intruder in your house by throwing a load of wet laundry down the stairs on top of him, just like in your book *That Wraps It Up*?"

I groaned. I wanted to slide right under my desk, right out of the room and right off the face of the earth.

Mom laughed. "No, thank goodness," she said. "But that story is a perfect example of how truth can be turned into fiction."

The buzzing in my head and the churning of my stomach kept me from hearing what I knew she was telling them. That she'd gotten that idea when I'd thrown my laundry over the railing, not knowing Grandpa was in the hall below, and the weight of it had knocked him down.

The questions, and the answers, could go on and on. About how I had caused a flood in my aunt's house by trying to flush my baby cousin's diaper down the toilet. And how I had killed my turtle by giving him a bubble bath.

Then it was time for art class. Mom left. I'd never been so glad for morning specials in my life.

When we got back to the room, Mrs. Perkins made us write thank-you notes to Mrs. Ryan and asked me to deliver them. She doesn't have to know that I shoved mine in the bottom of my backpack and have no intention of giving it to my mom. It read:

DEAR MRS. RYAN,

THANKS FOR RUINING MY LIFE.

YOUR SON,
HARVEY

P.S. I THINK IT'S REALLY PITIFUL THAT
AN AUTHOR COULDN'T COME UP WITH
A MORE INTERESTING NAME FOR HER
ONLY SON THAN HARVEY.

TWO

YOU NAME IT

Of course I know how I got my name. Harvey is Mom's maiden name, and since she didn't have any brothers and her dad didn't have any brothers, Mom decided to pass the family name along through me. I probably should be happy her name wasn't Darling, or Hickey, or Valentine.

Not only is my first name the same as Grandma and Grandpa's last name, but I look like Grandpa Harvey too. Not bald and bent over, but I have his brown eyes and the same brown hair that he used to have. Grandma says I have the same build Grandpa had in his younger days too. That must mean he was average in height and weight. I'm not the tallest or heaviest in my class, but I'm no shrimp. I guess I'm average all the way around. And average isn't what I want to be.

I have nothing against my grandpa, but how many eleven-year-old boys do you know named Harvey? How many baseball greats have been named Harvey, or even writers of great kids' books? Why couldn't I have a major-league name like Roberto, or Lenny? Or Jake? I'm going to need a major-league name about ten years from now.

Seal's mom named Seal after an old song, like from the sixties, by these old singers named Simon and Garfunkel. Now *Garfunkel* is a name I'm glad I don't have. He was famous for a while, even strapped with a name like that, so I guess there is hope for me. But Simon was famous longer. That's understandable when you think about his name. I rest my case.

Seal's real name is Cecilia (like the song) Jane Spicer. That's a good name, but I like the name Seal even better.

I write stuff like this, and like the thank-you note to Mom that she'll never see, in my journal. Sometimes I share it with Seal. I don't care that she's a girl. She knows how I feel about Mom basing her stories on my life. How I feel about her taking every little thing I do and blowing it up big, and then having everybody think it's all true—and usually hilarious.

Most people think it would be great to be the main character in a book, but I bet they wouldn't like it one bit if the whole world knew they'd once mistaken a skunk for a cat, or dressed for clash day a week early. Or still cried sometimes because their dad isn't always good at keeping promises.

I sometimes have this feeling that kids want to be my friend because they think they'll end up in one of Mom's books. They probably do show up in her books all the time, but she's clever about changing names and stuff. At least when the characters aren't related to her.

Seal could care less whether she shows up in a book or not. She's always telling me not to worry about it either, but she understands how and why I do.

We were talking about this while we worked on our stamp collections after Mom's visit to school.

"At least your mom pays attention to you," said Seal, without looking up from the stamps spread out on the card table in my room. "Mine doesn't even know I exist. Especially since she married good old Pete."

I was fixing a stamp from Sweden onto a page in my Traveler Worldwide Stamp Album.

Seal gasped. "*That's* what we need to do."

"What?" I asked.

"Find her a husband! We need to get your mom married. Get her mind on something else."

"You think that would work?" It didn't sound like a super idea to me, but Seal looked as excited as if she'd just found an album full of first day covers.

"My mom hasn't paid any attention to me, or anything else, since she married good old Pete."

"Who could we hook her up with?"

"Too bad she didn't meet Pete before Mom did. She'd have her hands full."

"Does Pete have any bachelor brothers?" I asked without much enthusiasm. I *had* met good old Pete.

Seal set down the tweezers she'd been using to separate

stamps. She pulled off the hair band from around her ponytail and shook her long black hair loose. This matter deserved her full attention. "I don't think so. But Mr. Stevens is unattached."

"He's *what?* That sounds painful!"

Seal's mom had lots of boyfriends before she settled down, for better or worse, with good old Pete. So Seal had lots of relationship words in her vocabulary that she was always having to explain to me.

"Unattached, silly. It means he doesn't have a wife or girlfriend. He's available. And he and your mom looked good together in the hall the other day, like they matched. I bet they have a lot in common, too. They both have kids in their jobs."

"But he's also our *principal.* Are you out of your mind? I can see the next book now—*The Boy with the Principal Dad.* Besides, he must be a lot older than Mom. She's only in her mid-thirties, and he's at least forty."

Seal shrugged. "Once you get old like that, a few years doesn't make much difference."

As soon as Seal left, I added this conversation to my journal. Of course I didn't take her seriously. At least not that night. And not about Mr. Stevens.

See, I think both my parents are great. But they aren't great together. I know they were young when they got married.

Mom was born and raised in Pennsylvania. She

moved to a little town in New York State right after college when she landed a job as a reporter for the local newspaper. One of her new coworkers invited her to a triple-A baseball game in a neighboring city. On the mound that night was Jake Ryan, a promising young pitcher who grew up in the town where Mom had just moved. She met him after the game and decided to write a local interest piece on him for the newspaper. The rest, so they say, is history. Mom and Jake Ryan, my dad, were married before the end of baseball season.

After I was born, Mom quit the newspaper so she could stay home with me. That's when she started to work seriously on her dream of writing books for kids. She wasn't an overnight success. I had to get old enough to do stupid things before she started to have kid appeal.

Dad's dream never came true. He was never called up to the major leagues. He didn't even have a "cup of coffee" in the majors. That's what they call it when a player is called up for a very short time. He was still pitching triple-A ball when he and Mom split up. He stopped dreaming a few years ago, settled down, and opened a tavern on Cayuga Lake.

When he was traveling with his team, Dad sent me postcards and letters and stuff. That's when I started collecting stamps. Now that he's in one place, I spend every other weekend and some extra days during the summer with him and his new wife, Mindy.

I don't think Mom likes Mindy. I've noticed she

doesn't open her mouth when she says her name. But I think Mindy is awesome. She helps at the bar at Dad's place. She's tiny and wears lots of gold jewelry. She looks about twenty. And she and my dad are crazy about each other. They really are. They love to go to ball games together, and golf, and bowl, and ski, and all kinds of things my mom never has time to do. Mindy's easy to talk to, and we have fun when we're together.

But this isn't about Dad and Mindy, or even them and me. It's about me and Mom, and how I wish she'd stop sharing me with the whole world, and stop carrying that little notebook around everywhere we go.

THREE

PLAY BALL

Usually my mom works normal hours like everybody else. But sometimes I wake up during the night and hear her clicking away on her keyboard. That sound is a nightmare to me because I know it means inspiration has struck. I spend the rest of the night worrying about what she's writing about. The night after Seal and I worked on our stamp collections was one of those nights.

The next morning I met Seal on the corner of Fulton and James, the midway point between my house and her apartment. We meet there so we can walk to school together. Seal noticed I hadn't slept much.

"You look beat. Did you stay up late working on your stamps?"

I had to finish a yawn before I could answer. "I wish. I woke up in the middle of the night and could see the glow from Mom's monitor under her study door. I was up the rest of the night. Which of my latest deeds could she be writing about? I haven't done anything stupid lately, have I, Seal? I mean, not since I heated up that dish of dog food thinking it was hash."

"You worry too much."

"I know, but I used to *love* hash. We don't even own a dog. What was that dog food doing in our fridge?"

"I told you yesterday, the solution to your problem is as simple as making dinner reservations for two."

"I don't know. Maybe. I *am* pretty tired. We're playing baseball at recess today, and I'm afraid I won't even be able to throw the ball across home plate."

"Work with me, boy." Seal patted me on the back.

Just then Brian Bartholomew, the other good pitcher in our grade, rode up on his bike. Almost everybody calls Brian "Bart." In private, Seal and I call him something else. I won't write it though, because Mom said never to put anything in print that you aren't willing to read out loud to your grandmother. No wonder so many kids don't want to write.

Anyway, Bart spun around us in circles as we continued to walk. "Hey, Lover Boy," he said to me, because I'm friends with Seal, "ready to get creamed this afternoon?"

"It's been a ong winter. I'm ready for you to try."

"Hope that pitching arm of yours isn't still in hibernation."

"Unlike you, I don't sleep through the winter," I shot back. I practice with my dad every time we get together, no matter what the weather is like. I didn't say that to Bart.

Brian ignored me. He started singing, "Cecilia, you're breakin' my heart—" as he rode away.

"That's not all I'll break, Brian!" Seal hollered after him.

Bart laughed.

Seal turned her angry gray eyes in my direction. "I'd like to open a can of whoop 'em on that bubble-brained boy," she said.

"Don't mind him. He's all talk," I told her. But I always felt a little uneasy around him. And I knew he was more than talk. Our best summer-league games were the ones against his team when he and I pitched against each other. No doubt his dad would coach his team again this year. My coach from last year had moved away, and I was hoping we'd find somebody as good as Mr. Bartholomew.

During the past couple of days the weather had warmed up enough and the fields had dried out enough that we could play ball during recess and gym. Our first summer-league practice was still two months away. I could hardly wait. In fact, it was hard to wait till recess that afternoon. My conversation with Bart had warmed up my blood, and I didn't feel tired anymore.

Fifth-grade recess is right after lunch. When Mrs. Perkins picked us up from the cafeteria she said, "Harvey, Mr. Stevens needs to see you. You can go to his office now and meet us on the playground when you're finished."

When I'm *finished*? I didn't even want to start. And couldn't whatever it was he wanted wait until after recess, until *after* I beat Brian Bartholomew?

Kids around me were saying, "Oooh, Harvey. What did you do?" and "You're in trouble now!" I could tell by the look of awe on Bethany's face that the possibility of me being in trouble made me even more interesting to her.

Seal poked me in the ribs. "Don't keep Mr. Stevens waiting," she said. "Think of your future."

The only future I wanted to think about was that ball game. Mr. Stevens had better make this quick.

The cafeteria is right across from the main office, so it didn't take me long to get there. When I did, Mom's friend the secretary smiled, asked how Mom was, then instructed me to have a seat in one of the plastic chairs lined up against the wall like a row of garbage cans on trash day. She turned back to her paperwork.

I didn't feel like hanging around. Not just because of the baseball game starting any minute, but also because everybody who came in and out of the office would think I was in trouble.

This sort of thing wouldn't bother Seal at all. She would love the chance to spy on staff members coming in to use the phone, pick up their mail, or make copies of homework sheets.

I could see Mr. Stevens talking on the phone in his office and took a hard look at him, like I was seeing him for the first time. I realized he looked a lot like Al Gore and was surprised no one had mentioned this to me before.

He was friendly like Mr. Gore seemed to be, too. Every Friday he invited two or three kids to eat lunch with him in his office. I'd been there a couple times, but not this year. One time I was called to his office because I'd witnessed a fight. He was tough, but fair.

Mr. Stevens was laughing on the phone and leaning back in his chair like he was really relaxed. This must not be one of those calls principals have to make to parents when kids are suspended or something.

He looked polished up, like he'd just had a bath and put on his best clothes. I tried to picture the guy in shorts, or swim trunks, or a baseball uniform, and I couldn't do it. I might as well have tried to imagine him with a surfboard in his hands or rolling to school on in-line skates.

He must have noticed me sitting there while my mind was wandering. I heard his deep voice call, "Come on in, Harvey."

I jumped up quickly and almost knocked the chair over. The friendly secretary barely noticed. She must see a lot of clumsy kids in her line of work.

"I have some dates written on a paper here," Mr. Stevens said. I looked around while he shuffled through papers on his desk. On his office walls were educational posters, pictures kids had drawn, and a large photo of an elderly couple, a young lady, and two kids. Mr. Stevens was in the picture, too.

"Here it is." He handed the paper to me. "These are some dates I've come up with that would work for a visit from your mom to the entire fifth grade. Hopefully one of them will fit into her schedule. She can send a note back to school with you."

This is what you called me in for? I thought. We're in the age of technology. *E*-mail her, *fax* her, pick up the phone and *call* her, for crying out loud. But don't make me miss recess. Especially when we're playing baseball!

"Okay," I said. "Can I go now?"

"Sure." Mr. Stevens laughed. "See you tomorrow."

I stuffed the paper into my pocket and hurried down the hall to the doorway by the baseball diamond.

Bart was coming off the mound, and my class was taking the field. My teammates cheered when they saw I'd made it out in time to pitch.

"Two to nothing, our favor," Bart said as he handed me the ball.

"Time to even the score then," I said.

My first pitch was in there for a strike, and my whole team cheered again. I threw two more in a row, and the first batter was down on strikes. The next batter popped one up and Amanda caught it for an easy second out. The third batter dribbled one down the first-base line. Our catcher went after it and threw it down to first for the third out. I'd held them at two runs. Now we had to score—at least twice—before it was time to go inside.

Bart's first pitch to this kid in my class named Trevor was a ball. His next pitch was right in there, and Trevor drilled it into left field for a double. Now we had a man on second base and no outs! This was looking good.

The next batter came to the plate. He wiggled around for a minute getting his stance just the way he wanted it, then stood there and didn't move a muscle. Bart threw three beauties right across the plate, and the kid went down on strikes. He didn't even swing.

Matt came up to bat, and Trevor hollered, "Send me home, Matty!"

Bart threw a ball in the dirt, and Matt watched it roll by for ball one. Matt watched the next ball go by too. Problem was, that one was a strike. He hit the next two foul, then popped one up right into the first baseman's glove. We were down to our last out, and I was afraid recess would end before we even scored one run, let alone the two we needed to tie.

"Come on, Mandy," I said to the next batter. "We can't leave Trevor stranded on second base."

Amanda didn't let me down. She connected with the first pitch Bart threw to her and sent the ball over the playground fence for a two-run homer! Trevor yoohooed all the way home from second base. Everyone on my team gave Amanda high fives. Bart just stood on the mound shaking his head.

Then Mrs. Perkins blew the whistle. Recess was over.

FOUR

OPERATION RESERVATION

I'd told Seal all about my trip to the office by the time we reached the corner of Fulton and James after school. "Can you believe he called me to the office for a *note*? Doesn't he know that passing notes in school is against the rules?"

"I'm telling you, this could be a good thing," Seal said. "We need to keep them in close contact."

"I don't see how we'd ever be able to make them want to date. I'm not sure I *want* to."

"It's not like they're mortal enemies. We've got something to work with here. Come over to my place. We'll plan our strategy—that's a game plan—and have a root beer float." Seal started off in the direction of her apartment.

"I know what a strategy is," I said. Seal knows how much I love root beer floats, but I didn't make any move to follow her.

She turned back to look at me. "Are you coming?"

I didn't answer.

"Pete's not home," she said.

"Oh, all right. And it doesn't make any difference to me whether Pete's home or not. I'm not afraid of him. He's just weird."

"You could do a lot worse for a stepfather. That's why we have to grab Mr. Stevens while we have the chance."

After we dropped our backpacks on Seal's floor, Seal sharpened two pencils and searched for a notebook. I took two frosty mugs out of the freezer, plopped in scoops of vanilla ice cream, and poured the root beer on top. Foam bubbled over the edges, and I quickly licked the sides of both mugs.

I'm not afraid of Pete. But I wouldn't have felt comfortable making the floats if he'd been home. Seal's apartment had felt like a second home to me before her mom got remarried. I felt awkward now that Pete lived there, like I was invading his space or like an uninvited guest. Did Seal feel like that in her own home? Would I feel like that in my house if Mr. Stevens, if *any* guy, moved in?

I called Mom to tell her where I was and that I'd be home in time for supper.

"I don't believe it," I exploded after I hung up the phone. "Mom said she's looking through my stamp albums and collector's magazines to help her with a story idea she's working on. I'll probably find her reading my journal next! This has to stop."

Seal simply nodded and waved the notebook in the air.

"You're right," I said. "We need to work on our game plan, and our game plan needs to work."

I pulled a folding chair up to the corner of Seal's desk.

"All right," she said. "I think it would be helpful if we list the things we know about Mr. Stevens's habits."

"Okay, but what for?"

"If we know what he likes and where he goes, it will be easier to stick them together. We'll be able to arrange *coincidental* meetings."

"I can barely arrange for the pizza boy to find our house when he's making a delivery." I laughed and felt some root beer go up my nose.

Seal stared at me over her float. "I'll be the note taker," she said as she put a heading on the top of a page: "Things We Know about Mr. Stevens."

"We know he wants to hear back from Mom," I said.

"Good." Seal wrote that down after #1.

"We know he has an office, and a friendly secretary, and he's not married, and his dog has fleas."

Seal laughed, but she didn't write anything down. "We don't even know if he has a dog," she said.

"My point exactly. What do we really know about this guy?"

Seal chewed on the pencil eraser. "I know he goes to the bakery every Saturday morning at eight o'clock. He's always in there reading the paper when I go down to pick up Pete's jelly doughnuts."

Seal scribbled away after #2.

I tried to think of times I'd seen Mr. Stevens. He was returning a movie to the video store once when Mom and I were picking up video games. I saw him mailing packages at the post office before Christmas. I thought I saw him pull up to McDonald's once, but when the person got out of the car, it was a tall homely lady instead.

"He's at school all the time," I said. "If you go in early to finish an assignment, he's there. If you stay late for an activity, he's there. Once I went over to school on a Saturday, hoping a custodian or somebody would let me in to get my math book. And you know who let me in? Mr. Stevens. It's like the guy has no life. Every time anybody is in that building, he's there. Like he lives in it."

"Yeah. And he's there for every game, concert, program, meeting. You name it. Hey, the spring chorus and band concert is Thursday night. He'll be there to give his welcome speech, and then he'll sit in the front row and watch the whole show."

"You'd think he'd get sick of it," I said. "What are you squirming around for?"

"My concert! You have to bring your mom to my concert and sit in the front row!"

"Nobody, except Mr. Stevens, ever sits in the front row."

"Exactly!" Seal flipped to a clean page in her notebook. "We have plenty of information to set our plan in motion."

I leaned over and watched her write "The Game Plan" across the top of the page. "Now what are you going to write? Where do we begin?"

"Let's start with what happened today. You know Mr. Stevens is expecting to hear from your mom, right?"

"Yeah, but . . . I've *got* it." I shook both my fists in the air. "When I give Mom the list of dates, I could say Mr. Stevens wants her to stop by his office to discuss them! She doesn't know he's only expecting a note back."

"Now your brain is working, Harv." Seal wrote:

#1 TOMORROW. SEND MOM TO THE OFFICE.
#2 THURSDAY NIGHT. SIT MOM IN THE VERY
    FIRST ROW.

Seal's pencil was doing all the work. I picked mine up and started to drum on the edge of her desk.

"Now what?" she asked.

"The bakery! I'll tell Mom she has to take me to the bakery Saturday morning."

"You're never up by eight on Saturday mornings," Seal reminded me.

"I'll tell her I'm turning over a new leaf. I'm going to

get up and . . . clean my room like she's been bugging me. But first I'd like to go to the bakery, just her and me, and try those jelly doughnuts I keep hearing about!"

Seal hooted. "You're a pure genius." She wrote,

#3 SATURDAY. 8 A.M. THE JELLY DOUGHNUT DATE.

Seal undid her ponytail and shook her hair loose. "Now we need to see how the game plan works. Once we see how this week goes, we'll make new plans for next week."

"But we're only in the first inning," I said. "We're striking out every batter that comes to the plate. We can't quit now!"

"We have to take our turn at bat. And keep score. We'll meet back here toward the end of the weekend to plan our strategy for the rest of the game."

I laughed. "Okay, but what are we going to call this operation? It has to have a name."

"You don't have any more reservations—that means doubts, Harv—about helping them discover they were made for each other?"

"I know what reservations are," I said. "They are also something you make to go out to dinner. Out to dinner on a *date*. And reservation rhymes with operation."

And then we both said together, "Operation Reservation!"

FIVE

FRONT-ROW SEATS

"I don't understand why you can't take a note back to Mr. Stevens for me," Mom said, tossing the salad so forcefully that I was surprised it stayed in the bowl. I'd given her the list of dates and told her Mr. Stevens wanted to see her the next day.

"I *can* take a note back, Mom. But I think he needs to see you to work out the details."

Mom didn't say anything. I know she doesn't like to have her work schedule interrupted.

"I'm just a kid, what do I know about planning these assemblies? But he better not be mad at me if you don't show up tomorrow." I walked to the fridge, partly to pour myself another glass of juice, but mostly so she wouldn't be able to see that I was almost laughing.

"For heaven's sake. It's not a big deal. I'll drive you to school tomorrow and see Mr. Stevens."

"I better call Seal and tell her I won't be walking with

her." I headed toward the phone, then paused. "Could we take her so she doesn't have to walk alone?"

"There are dozens of other kids walking—oh, forget it. Yes, we can pick up Seal on our way. But don't stay on the phone. It's time to eat."

Seal answered the phone after one ring. "Seal," I said loudly so Mom could hear, "my mom has a meeting or something with Mr. Stevens tomorrow. Want a ride to school?"

"So, she took the bait, eh, Harv?"

"Hook, line, and sinker," I whispered. "I may have discovered something else I'm good at."

"You'll have another chance to find out when it's time for my concert."

"I can hardly wait," I said in a conversational tone. "See you tomorrow."

"Thanks for the ride, Mrs. Ryan," Seal said as she climbed out of our car the next morning. Mom had parked in the visitors' lot at school. She was still in the car getting her appointment book from her briefcase.

"No problem at all," Mom replied.

"Your mom seems cheerful this morning," Seal observed. She was trying to tighten up her ponytail as we walked toward the school. I held her backpack for her.

"Once she adjusts to a change in plans, she's okay about it. It's best not to surprise her at the last minute.

She never minds my weekends at Dad's as long as they're on the calendar, but if he wants to do something with me that isn't planned ahead of time, she gets a little cranky."

We were by the bike rack outside the front door. Bart was chaining his ten-speed. "Feeling a little tired this morning, lovers? Had to have your mommy bring you? She drove right past me without asking if *I'd* like a ride. But I'm not the little star of her storybooks, am I?"

"What can I say, Bart? She only cares enough to bring the very best." Usually I kept my smart-alecky remarks to myself, but Bart was someone who begged me to share them. His comments were the kind that hurt me the most, but I refused to let him see that. Just like when I was pitching, I couldn't show the other team that I was rattled.

Bart laughed. "If she'd only *write* about the very best, her books would be about me instead of you!"

In a baseball game, no matter how far behind I am, I don't want the game to be over until I've won. But in real life I know it's better sometimes to settle for a tie score. We walked away from him.

"I'd like to punch his lights out," Seal stormed.

"You and me both," I said hotly. "But I'm saving my energy to make this his most miserable baseball season. That's my goal for the year."

"*One* of your goals," Seal reminded me.

———

Seal and I walked to my house after school. Mom was making dinner.

"All right, manicotti!" I said, seeing her stuff ricotta cheese mixture into big fat noodles. My day had improved after school started. First I beat Bart during recess, and now manicotti.

Mom only takes time to cook when she's completed a writing project or is struggling with a writing project. When she's working hard on a story, we eat a lot of salad, deli meat sandwiches on hard rolls, and stuff I can zap in the microwave. I'm not complaining! I love food, all food except hash, but anything Italian is my favorite. And those yummy buddy burgers Dad grills at his tavern.

Judging by the happy expression on Mom's face, I decided she must have finished a project or had good news from her editor. I wondered what the world would learn about me now. Some silly third-grader had asked for my autograph in the cafeteria!

"How'd things go with Mr. Stevens?" I asked, trying to sound like I really didn't care.

"Oh, fine. He's a nice man. Not at all like the principal of *my* elementary school. What an old grouch he was. Of course, times have changed since I was a girl." Mom laughed. Seal and I rolled our eyes at each other.

"Did you know that Rob—Mr. Stevens, I mean—used to be a history teacher?" Mom asked us. She wiped her hands on her apron. "I've always loved history."

"Me too, Mom. When's the manicotti going to be done?"

"We'll eat at five." Mom poured chunky tomato sauce over the stuffed pasta. "You're welcome to join us, Seal."

Seal called home and left a message with good old Pete while I set the table for supper. Then we went on-line for some information on ordering Babe Ruth and Wade Boggs stamps while we waited for the manicotti to come out of the oven. Mom called us at exactly five o'clock.

As Seal scooped up her second helping, she said, "I have a concert Thursday night, Mrs. Ryan. My mom's probably working." Seal shot a look at me as if I would forget our plan and blurt out that her mom never works on Thursday nights. "Do you think you and Harv could come?"

"That would be lovely, don't you think so, Harvey?"

"Oh, yes. Simply maa-velous!"

Seal nudged her foot against mine under the table. She was probably worried that if I acted too excited about going to her concert, Mom would be suspicious.

Thursday after school Mom was in her office. I tapped softly on her door to tell her I was home. "Seal's concert's tonight," I said through the door, but I was sure she wouldn't need the reminder.

"I'll be out soon. Sandwiches for supper."

I was piling smoked turkey breast and provolone cheese onto sesame seed buns when Mom came into the kitchen. "I want to be there early enough to sit in the front row," I said, then licked pickle juice off my fingers.

"Why in heaven's name would you want to sit in the first row, and why would we have to be there early to do it? They're terrible seats." Mom lifted the top buns off our sandwiches and slid in slices of tomato and lettuce.

"I want Seal to see us there rooting for her. I don't want her to have to search the stands to find us. We're her biggest fans!"

"We're going to a concert, Harvey. Not a baseball game. And nobody ever sits in the front row."

"Exactly! That's why they're such good seats." Mom looked confused. I'd scored another run.

When we were trying to leave the house, a magazine editor called Mom, wanting permission to print part of *The Skunk Who Came for Dinner* in an upcoming issue. Cripes, I thought, doesn't he realize every kid who likes to read has already read the whole thing?

I wanted Mom to hurry up the whole way to the concert. I didn't say anything, but I must have wiggled around a lot. She told me I should have used the bathroom before we left the house.

We made it to the concert just as Mr. Stevens was starting his welcome speech. Mom tried to sit toward the back, but I urged her forward to the seats in the empty first row. "Mom, I promised Seal we'd be up front!" She reluctantly tagged along.

Mom was right about one thing. Those front-row seats are terrible. I never did see Seal because the big old piano was parked right in front of my face. When Mrs. Potter, the chorus director, turned between each number and bowed to the audience, I got smacked in the nose with a strong perfumey-scented breeze.

One other thing I noticed between each number was that Mom and Mr. Stevens, who'd done what Seal and I had hoped and sat down by Mom after his speech, had their heads bent together chatting while they applauded. I wondered if Seal could see them. I could hardly wait to tell her.

"What an entertaining evening," Mom said on the way home. "I'm glad Seal's mom was able to be there after all."

"Seal's mom was there?" I asked in my best surprised voice. "*I* didn't see her."

Mom turned the corner onto our street. "Have you and your father worked out what time he's picking you up for the weekend?"

"I'm going to Dad's *this* weekend?" Operation Reservation had been going so well that I had forgotten. Now we'd have to put off the bakery visit for a whole week. What if Mom and Mr. Stevens lost interest in each other by then?

"You sound disappointed. I thought you liked going to your dad's."

"I do," I said quickly. "Seal and I had some plans is all. They can wait."

"If it ever becomes a problem for you to go away every other weekend, we need to talk it out with your dad." Mom sounded concerned. She came to a sudden stop in our driveway that jolted me forward.

"No, everything's okay." Man, I thought, keeping adults happy is a full-time job.

SIX

THE DATING GAME

The light was flashing on the answering machine when we returned from the concert. I hit the play button, listened as the little motor whirred into action, then heard, "Harv, it's Dad. I wish you were home, Buddy. Listen, something important has come up, and I have to cancel for most of the weekend. Call me at the tavern. Maybe we can work out something for Sunday afternoon. Sorry, Les. Sorry, Bud. Love you. 'Bye." I could hear laughter from the bar and glasses clinking in the background.

Ordinarily I'd be upset by a message like that. But that night I had to keep myself from shouting, "All right!"

Mom was biting her upper lip. I could tell she was trying hard not to say something. She wanted Dad and me to have a good relationship. I knew she had to work hard lots of times not to say bad things about him.

I also knew she'd be wanting to do something special with me to make up for the disappointment.

"Bummer," I said, in a let-down kind of voice.

"I guess you and Seal will be able to do whatever it is you had planned for this weekend." She gave me a quick hug.

"Yeah." Then I brightened. "How about you and me waking up early Saturday and going to the new bakery? Everybody has been talking about how good the doughnuts are, and I'd love to try them."

"It's a date," Mom said.

And I thought, If only you knew.

It was too late to call Seal, but I did call Dad. He apologized and said he and Mindy had a meeting at a golf course. Yeah right, I thought. Who has meetings at golf courses? But I didn't let it upset me because they still wanted to see me. Dad said they would pick me up Sunday afternoon and take me to a triple-A baseball game and out to dinner at the Steak Shack. If a genie had granted me three wishes for the weekend, I couldn't have asked for anything better than that. And I didn't even have to promise Mom I'd clean my room.

At 7:30 Saturday morning I hauled my hind end out of bed, thinking this better not be the day Mr. Stevens changed his Saturday routine, and those doughnuts better be the best I'd ever tasted.

It was 8:05 when the bells on the bakery door tinkled to announce our arrival.

I saw two things as I walked in: Seal, grinning and sitting alone at a table for two in the corner, and Mr. Stevens sitting alone at a table by the window, reading the morning newspaper. He glanced up when we came in. "Harvey, Leslie, how nice to see you. I'd be delighted if you'd join me." He folded the paper and set it aside.

"Seal's here all by herself, Mom. I'll sit with her, but you can sit with Mr. Stevens."

There was an awkward moment when I could tell Mom was confused about whether or not she and I should be separated on our "date." This had not been part of her plan.

"Okay," she said at last, handing me a five-dollar bill. "Buy yourself a couple doughnuts and something to drink. And bring me back an Irish cream coffee, please. And the change."

"I'll buy your coffee, Leslie. I was about to refill my mug," Mr. Stevens offered.

I made a line drive toward Seal before Mom could object, as Mr. Stevens headed to the counter. I had to stop myself from cheering.

"Try to act natural, Harv," Seal whispered.

As soon as Mr. Stevens sat down with Mom, I strolled up to the counter and asked for three doughnuts—a jelly and a chocolate cream for me, and a lemon-filled doughnut for Seal.

Seal sank her teeth into her doughnut, and yellow filling oozed out. I took a bite of mine and hit jelly right away. "Ummm, ummm, ummm. Pete may have his faults, but he knows how to pick a doughnut."

Seal and I snuck little glances at the table by the window. Mr. Stevens had apparently convinced Mom to try a doughnut. He was brushing powdered sugar off her chin.

"How romantic," whispered Seal. "Pete would have said, 'Marge, get that stuff off your face. You look like a clown.'"

We giggled. Mom and Mr. Stevens looked over at us and smiled. We waved. Then we did our best to ignore them while I told Seal about an article I'd read on the new Olympic stamps being issued by the United States Postal Service.

When we finished eating, I handed over Mom's change and told her I was going with Seal to deliver Pete's doughnuts.

"Harvey," Mom said, "Mr. Stevens has invited me to attend a lecture on the Underground Railroad that's being given at the historical society this afternoon. I told him that you already had plans with Seal and that I'd be happy to join him. Okay?"

Mom sure *looked* happy to join him. "Yeah, sure," I practically stuttered. "Plans, yeah, we have plans."

The bells jingled again as Seal and I left the bakery.

"Do you realize what this means?" Seal asked, grabbing my arm.

"Yeah, my mom has a date! She's not going to be

home working on a Harvey story. She's going somewhere with Mr. Stevens!"

"I can't believe we did it so easily. And so quickly! We're good, Harv. Really, really good. We could go into the matchmaking business, we're so good."

"Yeah," I quipped, "too bad we weren't in business when *your* mom needed help."

"My mom never needed help finding men," Seal reminded me, "just getting rid of them."

After Seal and I handed over the doughnuts, we spent the rest of the morning, which turned out to be drizzly, organizing our first day covers in their notebooks and playing computer baseball.

I was back home, sitting in front of the TV and writing the week's amazing events in my journal, when Mom arrived home from the historical society. She didn't look at all like she usually does when her day has been interrupted by something unexpected.

"Harvey, that was the most fascinating lecture I've been to in ages. I had no idea local homes had been part of the Underground Railroad. I took pages of notes. Then Rob—Mr. Stevens—loaned me some books he has on the subject and showed me photographs he's taken of historic homes. He's not only a historian but a decent photographer as well!" Mom held the books tight to her, as if they might be stolen if she put them down.

"Maybe I could look at those books sometime. I've been interested in the Underground Railroad ever since we studied it in fourth grade. Did they talk about how close our town is to where Harriet Tubman lived?"

"Yes. And I also learned from Rob that the fifth-grade teachers have filed requests to go on field trips to Auburn to visit Harriet's home and grave site in a few weeks."

"Great! My fourth-grade class never went to Auburn last year because that stupid blizzard canceled our trip. Remember that?"

Mom nodded. "I'd be interested in chaperoning that trip." She finally put the books down on the coffee table. "I've been thinking about taking a break from fiction," she added. "This might be the nonfiction material I've been waiting for."

"Great idea!" I didn't figure there was any way I could end up in a book about Harriet Tubman and a bunch of dead guys, even though my town *had* been on the Underground Railroad route. I picked up one of the books and leafed through it. Seal, I thought, we are very, very good.

SEVEN

IS THAT A PROMISE?

When Dad and Mindy picked me up for the ball game Sunday afternoon, Mom was making an enormous batch of meatballs. She had invited Mr. Stevens over for supper. I was glad I'd be gone. Spaghetti is much better left over.

We stopped at the Steak Shack on our way to the game. "So you're out there knocking the old ball around already?" Dad said after we'd settled into our favorite booth and ordered our steaks and fries.

"During recess and gym. We've won almost every game I've pitched, even against Bart. Remember him?"

"The Bartholomew kid? He was good competition for you last year."

"I'm a little worried about this year, because we haven't found a new coach for our team yet. And Bart says his dad will be coaching his team again."

"I'm sure you'll do fine. I wish I could help you out. I'd love to do some coaching."

"Would you really, Dad?" After my dream of playing major-league ball, I dreamed most about Dad coaching my team.

"Why don't you, Jake? I'd enjoy Harvey's games twice as much if both of my boys were on the team." Mindy winked at me.

Our server arrived with our salads. I shook Parmesan cheese on mine and waited for Dad's answer.

"I can't spend that much time away from the tavern, Min. Coaching is a big commitment."

"But it's not a full-time thing. It's only for the summer and not even every day," Mindy encouraged him.

"Yeah, Dad. School would be out, so you could hold daytime practices. Games are only one or two nights a week and never on Friday and Saturday, your busiest nights. You'd make it back by nine-thirty at the latest, anyway."

"Are you two ganging up on me?" Dad's eyes twinkled. "It's tempting."

"We've hired great help at the tavern," Mindy reminded him. "I'd be fine on practice days until you arrived. And you know how Benny likes to take over when we both go to games. Just do it. You know you want to." Mindy grinned.

"And *I* really want you to. You come to most of my games anyway. You wouldn't have to make extra trips to pick me up when I'm staying with you because I'd just go home with you after the game."

"Well, Bud, you may have yourself a deal."

"All right," I said, and Mindy gave me a high five. Man, I thought, I've really sharpened my persuasive powers over the last few days. Maybe I should consider a future in politics!

The game wasn't the best we'd ever seen. The home team, Dad's old triple-A team, lost by four runs. Dad said they'd improve after a few more games. The best action was in the bottom of the fifth inning when our lead-off batter hit a homer that tied up the game. Then they loaded up the bases, but couldn't bring another man home. The opposition brought in two runs in the sixth inning, and two in the ninth.

Dad explained to Mindy and me how each play came together and why it worked, or didn't. He'll be the best coach, I thought. I couldn't wait for Bart to find out.

When we were almost back to my house, I began to feel nervous. What if Mr. Stevens was still there? I didn't want to see him myself, and I didn't want Dad and Mindy to see him with Mom.

"Harvey, did you hear me?" Dad asked, and I realized I hadn't been paying any attention.

"Sorry. What did you say?"

"That one of our regular customers is a retired postal worker. He's collected stamps for nearly sixty years. He'll bring them to the tavern when you're around and show them to you."

"That would be super. Could we stop for ice cream?"

"Aren't you full *yet*? After that huge meal and snacks at the game, I'd think you'd be ready to burst! I know I am." Dad patted his stomach with one hand, keeping the other on the steering wheel.

"He's a growing boy, Jake. Of course we'll stop." Mindy turned and grinned at me. "I love ice cream. I was hoping you'd ask."

The ice cream stop only slowed us down ten minutes. They had me home much sooner than I wanted to be. And I *was* ready to burst.

As soon as the house was in sight, I leaned forward over the front seat so I could see if there was an extra vehicle in the driveway.

Mr. Stevens was gone.

Dad and Mindy stayed only a few minutes.

As soon as we were alone, Mom looked at her watch. "It's a good thing you did your homework last night."

"I know. I'm ready to crawl in bed and read."

"Me too." Mom yawned. "I planned to do some writing tonight to make up for not working this weekend, but I think I'll take Rob's Underground Railroad books upstairs and read till I fall asleep. That shouldn't take long." She yawned again. She was making me feel exhausted.

While I brushed my teeth I thought about what a great weekend it had been for me *and* for Mom. And about how weird it was that I hadn't wanted Dad and Mindy to see Mom with Mr. Stevens. Dad and Mindy had each other, so it shouldn't make any difference to them if Mom had a friend. And I would be happy if Mr. Stevens could just take her mind off writing about me.

EIGHT

READY OR NOT

Monday morning started like any other school day. Seal and I met on the corner and walked the rest of the way together. I wasn't ready for the greeting in store for me on the school playground. I could tell by the expression on Bart's face that he had been waiting for me to show up. He looked like he'd won a doubleheader and was bragging about it to anyone who would listen.

Bethany rushed up to Seal and me. "Is it true what Bart is telling everyone?"

"What's he saying?" I asked, feeling defensive before she answered.

"That your mom and Mr. Stevens are *dating*." The way she said "dating" made it sound like the most thrilling thing she'd ever heard. I had the same sinking feeling I get in that instant when I realize a guy has hit a home run off my pitch.

"Where did he come up with *that* idea?" I said.

"So you're saying it's not true?" I heard disappointment in her voice.

"Of course it's not true!"

"Then how come your face is all red?" Bethany leaned close, inspecting my cheeks. "Are you blushing, Harvey?"

I was attracting a small crowd, Bart among them. "You can't deny it, Harvey Ryan. My mom saw them together at the historical society on Saturday."

Seal laughed. "You call that a *date*? Brian, you're pathetic. Dates are supposed to be *romantic*, not . . . *historical.*"

Everyone in the group gathered around us laughed.

"Besides," I said, "your mom was there too. How do we know *she's* not dating Mr. Stevens?"

"Yeah, Bart," several people said in unison.

"Because my mom is *married*. To my *dad*."

"Then I don't think I'd go around announcing that she was at the historical society with Mr. Stevens." I pretended to be shocked. I was playing to the crowd, and enjoying the laughter at Bart's expense.

"She was *not* at the historical society with Mr. Stevens! She was just there." Bart's face was starting to look sunburned.

"What a coincidence. My mom was just there, too." I grinned at him innocently. He had the same look of confused disbelief that he gets when he strikes out. Most of the kids were shaking their heads at him.

Bart stamped his foot. "You idiots. My mom *saw* them together."

"So what?" Seal said, leaning forward with her hands on her hips. "My mom drives old Mr. Baker to church sometimes, and he sits with her in our pew. That doesn't mean they're dating."

"With *your* mom, anything is possible," Bart retorted.

"That's it. Now you've gone too far." I took a step toward Bart, but Seal held me back.

The last morning bell rang. Everybody had two minutes to go to their lockers and be in homerooms before attendance was taken.

"You going to fight Bart at recess today?" Trevor asked.

"He is *not.*" Seal answered before me. "Brian Bartholomew is immature and not worth the trouble."

"I fight my battles on the baseball field," I said.

I heard a few comments like, "You'll beat him then, Harv." But I also heard a couple people call me a chicken under their breath. I was glad Bart was in a different fifth-grade class. I wouldn't even see him until lunch and recess.

After morning announcements, Mrs. Perkins told us about the field trip to Harriet Tubman's home in Auburn the next week. Our class would be going. So would Bart's. "I'd like to take a parent chaperone from our class. Harvey, would you ask your mom if she'd be able to join us? Mr. Stevens thought she'd be interested."

I knew some of the kids were giving me strange looks, but I nodded anyway.

I watched the clock all morning. It was a very warm day for this early in the spring. I was nervous about seeing Bart at recess. There was no way I could let him beat me that day.

At lunchtime I avoided the table where Bart always sits. I never sit with him, but now I didn't even want to walk past him. Word had spread about our argument, and I could feel people looking in my direction while I ate.

Everybody acted wild like they do just before a vacation, and our lunch monitor had to keep quieting people down. Mr. Stevens must have heard the extra commotion from over in his office. I noticed him standing in the cafeteria doorway. I also noticed that I was gulping my food and forced myself to slow down.

"I can't believe you're going to ask your mom to go on the trip," Seal said. "You hate to have her tag along. Remember that little kids' story she wrote about you dressing up like a tiger after she went to the zoo with our kindergarten class?"

"True. But thanks to Mr. Stevens she's interested in history again, and I plan to keep it that way. She thinks she'd like to write something about Harriet Tubman. And I think *I'd* like her to write something about Harriet Tubman."

"Good plan." Seal peeled the lid off a carton of peach

yogurt. "Can you believe how well things are working out with your mom and Mr. Stevens?"

"Keep your voice down. I wouldn't exactly call what happened this morning 'working out well.' I think these kids expect me to fight Bart on the playground today. I don't want to do that. Do you know how embarrassing it would be to be sent to Mr. Stevens's office for fighting *now*?"

The fifth-grade teachers arrived, and kids lined up in the doorways to go outside for recess. Would I be able to save face without fighting Bart? My mouth felt as dry as if I'd just eaten third base instead of finishing off my lunch with a juice box.

Our teachers kept shushing us as we filed down the hall to the playground door. The buzzing turned to eager shouts as we broke into the bright sunlight, like bees that have been shut up in a box and are suddenly let loose.

Bart's team would be up first today because my team had first ups last time we'd played. But the players were droning around Bart and me waiting for something else to happen. I hoped I wasn't going to get stung.

"Let's play ball," I yelled above the noise.

"You chicken?" Bart asked.

"Not at all," I said, more bravely than I felt. I was sweating already. "You and your buddies could beat me up if you wanted to, but that doesn't prove anything. I think you're trying to stall the game because you don't want your team to lose again." Standing up to Bart was giving me a thrill a little like the one I feel when I'm pitching and I'm not sure how the batter will react to the ball hurtling toward him.

"We're ready when you are, punk." Bart slammed his fist into his baseball mitt. That was much better than him slamming it into my face.

Teachers seem to have a sixth sense whenever trouble is brewing. I noticed a couple of them heading toward our group as we scrambled for our playing positions.

Sweat was trickling down the back of my neck, and I'm not sure it was all from the heat. I don't think I'm a chicken, but I know I didn't want to fight. I was willing to give my brain a workout and save my fists the trouble. Dad had told me there's more honor in avoiding a fight.

I'd never wanted to beat Bart in a baseball game as badly as I did right then. It didn't start out well.

I hit their first batter in the ankle. He hobbled to first base while his teammates booed me. I got behind in the count on the next batter, then he dropped one into the outfield for a single. There were two runners on and nobody out.

I unstuck my shirt from my chest, wiped my greasy hands on my jeans, and struck out the next two kids that came to the plate. The next kid popped one deep into left field.

"I got it, I got it, I got it!" yelled Matt. But Matt

didn't have it, and two runners scored before we got control of the ball.

The next batter grounded out to short for the third out.

Bart took the mound, and he was flawless. Our first three batters went down on strikes, even Mandy.

I was back on the mound before I could catch my breath.

The second inning went as badly as the first. Between my pitching and my teammates' fielding, we really stunk up the field.

And Bart could do no wrong. The score was six–zip when recess ended.

After the whistle blew for us to line up, Bart pointed at me and said, "See, everybody, that's what a real loser looks like."

"I guess you've forgotten that you didn't win a single game last week," Seal reminded Bart.

Some of the kids, at least the ones in my class, laughed. Bethany kept laughing after everyone else stopped. Bart glared at her.

Then I remembered what I'd been eager to tell everyone that morning. The problem on the playground had put it out of my mind earlier. "Guess what my dad told me this weekend? He's going to coach my baseball team this summer."

A couple of kids who'd been on my team last summer started to chant, "Harvey, Harvey, Harvey." Other kids rolled their eyes. One kid yelled, "Hey, can I be on your team?" Bart punched him in the shoulder.

I was the last one in line at the drinking fountain. When my turn came, I bent over the spout for a long time, drinking in the cool liquid and calming my nerves.

Seal had to make up a music lesson after school. I hung around, waiting, shooting baskets on the playground with a couple of junior high boys until she came out of the building, because I needed to talk to her.

"I'm proud of you," she told me, handing me her clarinet. "You really put a roadblock in the middle of Bart's ego trip."

"By losing the game?"

"By being bigger than him even when you lose. Is your dad really going to coach your team this summer?"

"That's what he says. Listen, I made it through the rough spots today, but what's going to happen if Mom continues to see Mr. Stevens? I lied about it this morning. How long do you think I can keep that up? Why didn't we think about how the kids would act about them dating? I don't need this kind of attention. Everything is so complicated." My backpack felt as heavy as if I'd filled it with all my textbooks from the last two years. The handle on Seal's clarinet case was digging into my hand and making it sweat.

"Life is complicated, Harv. You can't let it worry you too much. The main thing is to keep your mom's focus off you. We'll be able to deal with anything else that comes along. Are you forgetting how good we are?"

"No, I'm not forgetting that. But I'm worried about the other things we might be forgetting. I had enough trouble planning my own life. Now I have to worry about Mom too."

NINE

LET THEM EAT CAKE

One thing I didn't have to worry about for a few days was facing Bart at recess. It rained the rest of the week, so baseball was out. For once that didn't bother me. If I was lucky Bart would forget about our disagreement by the time the sun came out.

One person who wasn't worrying about anything was Mom. She acted like she never had another deadline to meet. She cooked supper every night, trying new recipes. If she was writing, she was doing it while I was at school every day. She spent the evenings reading books on local history and the Underground Railroad. Her computer was quiet all night long.

What with that and all the rain, I should have been sleeping like a lazy old cat. But just about the time I crawled in bed each night the phone rang. I ran for it Monday night, but Mom called, "I've got it, Harv."

Who could it be, I wondered? I had a sneaking suspicion it was my school principal. And he wasn't calling to report on my behavior. I could hear her speaking softly and laughing every now and then until I fell asleep.

On Tuesday night she answered the phone in the middle of the first ring.

I was cranky Wednesday morning. "Who's calling you so late at night?"

"I'd hardly call nine at night 'so late.'"

"Well, it's past my bedtime." I shoved my homework into my backpack, bending back the cover on my science notebook.

Mom raised her eyebrows at me. "But not past *mine*," she reminded me, still not answering my question.

I thought she was being quite rude. But now I was sure Mr. Stevens was making the calls. She would have told me if it was Grandma, or her editor, or even Dad.

On Wednesday Mrs. Perkins made another announcement. She told us there was going to be a writing contest for the fifth grade. We were to create an interesting or humorous character, and make him or her sound like a real live person we would enjoy reading about. The entries would be judged by the fifth-grade teachers and my mom, and the winning character would appear in one of Mom's upcoming books.

Right away people wanted to know if we *had* to write something. There were several loud groans when Mrs. Perkins said yes, it was an assignment. The teachers had decided it would be good practice for the writing test that comes at the end of fifth grade, and the entries could be shown off with our other writing samples at the annual Young Authors' Day. This year Mom would speak at an assembly on Young Authors' Day and would announce the winning character.

If my mom didn't have anything to do with it, I would have enjoyed entering a writing contest. But she was butting in on my schoolwork. I groaned along with the others.

Not everyone was discouraged. Bethany said dreamily that she would write about a beautiful princess. I also heard aliens, monsters, basketball heroes, and evil teachers mentioned.

I thought I might write about an unbeatable pitcher with an awesome name or a kid who'd traveled to every country in the world and held the Guinness record for the largest stamp collection.

Seal decided she would probably write about the first woman president, or a female scientist who discovers a cure for the common cold. Seal is a complex person.

Wednesday was also the night the doorbell rang while I was doing my homework. I don't know who I expected to see when I opened the door, but I probably shouldn't have been surprised to find Mr. Stevens standing there.

"Mom," I hollered, after swallowing what felt like a fireball stuck in my throat, "it's for you!"

"Well, let him in," Mom said, coming up behind me.

"I should have called first," Mr. Stevens apologized. "I

was on my way home from a meeting and thought I'd stop for a few minutes. I hope you don't mind."

"Not at all," Mom insisted. She cleared her throat, and I realized I was still blocking the doorway.

I jumped out of the way quickly so he could come in. I didn't want anyone to see him standing on our porch!

"Do you have time for a cup of coffee?" Mom asked. "I made apple cake this afternoon. I'm sure Harvey would like another piece."

"In that case, I can't possibly refuse," Mr. Stevens said.

Mom directed us to the kitchen. She made coffee, and I took three small plates out of the cupboard. Mr. Stevens looked relaxed, and I remembered this wasn't the first time he'd been to our house.

I love apple cake, but I wasn't going to sit and chat with Mom and Mr. Stevens. "I'll take my cake to my desk. I'm studying my vocabulary words." I think it's probably a smart move for students to let teacher-type people know they're doing homework whenever they have a chance.

"Your mom tells me you are interested in the Underground Railroad." Mr. Stevens pulled a chair away from the table, the *head* of the table, so he could sit down.

"Yeah. I've been checking out your books, and I'm looking forward to our field trip next week."

Mr. Stevens nodded his head. "I'm looking forward to the field trip also."

"You . . . you're going on the field trip too?" I stuttered. " I . . . I mean, I didn't think principals had time to do stuff like that. Do you think you should spend so much time away from school?"

Mom and Mr. Stevens laughed.

"It has been a while. But I'm sure everyone at school will manage fine without me, and probably be happy to have me gone for a day."

Ha, ha, ha. The three of us laughed. I didn't feel hungry for the cake anymore, but I took a piece from Mom's outstretched hand and asked to be excused.

Of course I didn't head back to my desk. I headed straight for the phone.

"No way!" Seal said after I explained why I was calling. "What are they doing this very minute?"

"Eating their cake, I guess."

"Keep checking on them," she urged. "Write everything down so you don't forget to tell me anything."

"I can't spy on my mother!"

"Just *watch* them, Harvey. Go in the kitchen and ask for another piece of cake or something. Then go back a few minutes later to put your plate in the sink. Don't you remember any of the ways we used to keep an eye on my mom and her boyfriends?"

"Oh, good grief! What if I walk in and they're *kissing*?"

"I think your mom *and* Mr. Stevens, unlike some people whose names we won't mention, have more sense than that. And if you keep reminding them that you're around—Harvey, stop that moaning!"

"What if somebody sees his car in our driveway?"

"So what?" I could picture her shrugging on the other end of the phone line. "This isn't the first time you've ever had company. Most people probably don't know what kind of car Mr. Stevens has."

There wasn't much to write down for Seal other than what I'd told her on the phone. Mr. Stevens didn't stay long after he finished his cake. Who could blame him, what with me beeping in and out of the room every five minutes like the timer on a watch.

The only conversation I overheard was about the stupid field trip and the stupid Young Authors' Day assembly. I did walk in on them with their heads bent together looking at some pictures Mr. Stevens had brought, and it looked like *maybe* the ends of their fingers were touching on purpose. I was glad when he left.

As soon as he pulled out of the driveway, I remembered some important news I hadn't shared with Mom yet.

"Did I tell you that Dad is going to coach my summer-league team?"

She shook her head and sighed. "I wouldn't get my hopes up, Harv."

"You're always down on him!"

"Only when he hurts you."

"Well, he's not going to." I went off in a huff. I still hadn't looked at my vocabulary words.

———

There was at least one person who *did* know what kind of car Mr. Stevens had. He took a detour to my table the next day when he dumped his lunch tray so he could tell me he knew.

"How'd you enjoy your company last night, Harvey?" Bart had a wicked grin.

"What are you talking about?" I asked, hoping he couldn't hear my heart pounding. I didn't like sitting with him hovering over me.

"Come off it, Ryan. I saw Mr. Stevens's car in your driveway last night."

"The car? That belonged to my mom's Avon lady."

"The Avon lady has a black Blazer? How come I've never noticed it parked there before?"

"She's new. And what's so weird about her having a Blazer? My stepmom has one too," I lied.

Bart stormed off, shaking his head.

"I'm a liar," I whispered to Seal. "A big fat liar. And I can't stop! What is going to happen next week when they're together on our field trip?"

Seal shrugged. "They won't be holding hands."

"That's not funny."

"Sorry," she said. "You're just going to have to cross that bridge when you come to it."

"What do you mean, *I'm* going to have to cross that bridge? I thought we were a team?"

"We are. But there isn't anything we can do about it right now. Unless you want to end all the suspense this minute and admit to everyone that Mr. Stevens and your mom *are* seeing each other."

"No way! Never would be too soon for that."

TEN

CROSSING SOME BRIDGES

No matter how much you don't want some things to happen, there's no way to avoid them. Like that semiannual visit to the dentist, or a big math exam, or a field trip. Or word getting around about your mom and her boyfriend.

Mom and Mr. Stevens spoke on the phone right at my bedtime every night for the rest of the week. On Saturday night they had a *real* date. Not the historical kind, but to dinner and a play. I hoped Bart's nosy, gossipy mother didn't have reservations and tickets for the same places.

On Sunday, Dad and I made plans over the phone for the following weekend. I could hardly wait for some time with him at the lake. It'd be great to get away from Bart and Mom and Mr. Stevens for a couple days.

The sun was shining on Monday, but the fields were wet, so we stayed in for gym and played a game with foxtails, baseballs with long, colorful fabric "tails" sewn to them. I wasn't disappointed. We weren't outside, but playing with foxtails is a whole lot better than having to square-dance or some of the other indoor stuff we have to do.

We had to stay on the blacktop for recess. Bart was organizing a game of doctor dodge ball, so I decided to shoot hoops.

At the end of the day Mrs. Perkins posted the groups for our trip to Auburn. We were told to check and see which chaperone we'd been assigned to. Of course I found my name under Ms. Leslie Ryan. Seal's was under Mr. Rob Stevens.

Seal nudged my arm. "We can sit together anyway."

"Great. I wonder who Mom will sit with."

"The chaperones always sit together in the front seats. No one will think anything of it."

"Yeah, right," I said sarcastically. "No one will even notice."

The Monday-night phone call came right on schedule.

I would love to have awakened on Tuesday morning with strep throat, pneumonia, hives, even diarrhea—anything that came with a fever or lumps. But I felt depressingly healthy. And I knew better than to fake it. I lay in bed wishing for a miracle illness and wondered how I could convince Mom to stay home. It came to me as I heard her approach my door.

She knocked. "Time to get up. Today is our trip."

"Mom," I called to her from my bed, "did you see my note for you to call your editor?"

"What note?" She pushed my door open. "When was this?"

I propped myself up on one elbow. "Yesterday. Your editor called and wanted you to call her back. Didn't you see the note?"

"No, I didn't. Can you remember anything else she said?"

"Just that she needs you to call her back between ten and eleven this morning."

"I won't be here between ten and eleven. I'll have to call her before we leave. I have her home number." She started to close my door.

I sat bolt upright. "You can't do that! I mean—she said she wouldn't be home this morning. And she will only be in her office between ten and eleven."

Mom was back in my room. "That's very strange. I wonder what's going on. Guess I'll have to take the cell phone and call her from our trip."

"You can't. I mean—the batteries are dead."

"I charged them last night, Harvey. Not to worry."

That's what you think, I muttered to myself after she left. Not only was she still going on the trip, but now she'd be calling her editor and finding out she hadn't needed to.

I looked outside, hoping that one of those late-season blizzards, like the one that had canceled our trip last year, or a flood from last week's rain, was brewing outside my window. The sun was shining. Birds were chirping. Spring had sprung. Where's a natural disaster when you need it the most?

I had a brainstorm! I dressed quickly, hurried downstairs, and burst into the kitchen. "Mom, I'm expecting a special package of foreign stamps to arrive any day. What if they come today, and no one is here to receive them?"

"Stamps aren't that big. Even a package of them. I'm sure our mail carrier will be able to put them in our mailbox."

"But what if they don't fit? What if she just leaves them on the porch and they get wet or blown away or stolen?"

"What is the matter with you? You've never worried about our mail service before. If you hadn't asked me to come on this trip I'd think you were trying to keep me home today. You don't have a fever, do you?" She felt my forehead, which was as cool as a cantaloupe, shrugged her shoulders, then went to put on her makeup. I gave up.

We swung by Seal's apartment on our way to school.

Mom said she'd wait in the office until it was time to leave. In the past that is exactly where I would have wanted her, instead of hanging around my classroom. I know this isn't proper English, but I have to say it anyway. Ain't fate funny?

After we'd boarded the bus, Mr. Stevens stood up in the front. He looked like a Saint Bernard trying to squeeze into a Volkswagen. Everyone quieted down.

"Whenever students leave the school grounds, I hear reports of how well behaved you are. This kind of behavior is what enables us to continue these entertaining, educational trips. Let's remember that fine tradition by being respectful of each other, our hosts, and the places we visit. You're allowed to have fun if you follow the rules." He smiled. "One last thing. Keep it to a dull roar in here, and Mr. Bevins, our bus driver, will play that radio station you all seem to like." Everybody clapped and whistled. Mr. Stevens held up his hand for quiet. "If the noise level becomes deafening, we'll place chaperones in the back and middle of the bus and switch the station to classical music. It's your choice." Groans were heard all around, then the noise quieted to the level of a small farm tractor.

Seal and I, with our stack of stamp collectors' magazines, sat in the middle. We didn't want to be near Bart, who was in the backseat, or Mom and the rest of the chaperones occupying the first two seats. Of course Bethany was right behind Mom, and would have climbed in the seat with her if we'd had an uneven number of chaperones. Thinking about the occupants of the front seat, I was grateful that the high backs on the seats kept people from being able to see each other. Usually kids like the high seats because it's harder for the chaperones to see them. I liked the high seats because they made it harder for the kids to see the chaperones. I wondered if Bethany would overhear anything interesting.

After a fifty-minute bus ride that seemed more like five days, our first stop in Auburn was at Freedom Park, a memorial to Harriet Tubman and others for the work they had done to free so many slaves. We stood on the brick walkway that surrounds an engraved block reading "Harriet Tubman, 1820–1913, Moses of Her People," and read facts about her and the Underground Railroad on a glass-enclosed signboard. I wondered if Harriet had stood right on that very spot.

Then I stood by nervously while Mom called her editor's office. But it seems that the editor was out for the whole day and her secretary didn't know a thing about a phone call needing to be returned. It's hard to find good help these days.

After Freedom Park, we went to Fort Hill Cemetery, where Harriet is buried. It's a big cemetery full of hills and twisty roads. Even with directions, it took us a while to find her stone. Some of the kids thought it was creepy to be in a cemetery, but I thought about how special Harriet was to have so many people interested in where she's buried. Mrs. Perkins had brought a large roll of brown paper and special crayons so we could make rubbings of Harriet's stone.

Our last stop was the Harriet Tubman Home, where Harriet had lived and run a home for old black people after the Civil War. We saw a video about her life before we went through her house. Then a descendant of Harriet's led the tour! She knew even more than the video. Mom took notes the whole time. I knew they weren't about me for a change.

The house is small, so each of the four groups went in separately. While we waited for our turn, Mr. Stevens took our pictures standing on Harriet's porch. After everybody had been through, we brought bag lunches off the bus and sat in the grass behind the house to eat.

I was glad that the four chaperones sat together in a clump. Mom and Mr. Stevens didn't look like a couple that way. Actually, except for sitting together on the bus, they hadn't really done anything that made them look like a couple. I finally relaxed about both of them being on the trip. I remembered the days of Mom sitting on the bus with *me*.

Then Bart plopped himself down by my elbow. "Will Mr. Stevens be coming to all your baseball games this summer, Harvey?"

"Why would he do that?" So much for relaxing, but I tried to keep my voice calm.

"For the same reason he came on our field trip today. To be near your mom."

"He came with us today because he's very interested in the Underground Railroad and taking pictures of historic places."

"So now you're an expert on Mr. Stevens. What else is

he interested in? How does he spend his evenings and weekends? "

"Gee, Bart, I don't know. Maybe you should ask your mother."

I expected that to rile Bart, but all he did was laugh. "You know, Harvey, sooner or later you aren't going to be able to hide the truth. All the teachers will really love you then. Just wait till everybody finds out you're almost the principal's *stepson*."

Bethany had wandered over at the end of Bart's speech. "Oh, my gosh," she said breathlessly. "You're going to be Mr. Stevens's stepson?"

"No! No, I'm not!" I jumped up, dumping a bag of pretzels off my lap.

"You're not what, Harvey?" I hadn't seen Mom and Trevor walk over to us. Mom was helping him pass out cupcakes that his mom had sent with him to share for his birthday.

"Harvey, I asked you a question. You're not what?" Mom repeated.

I couldn't think of anything to say.

Good old Seal came to the rescue.

"He's not going to lead us in singing 'Happy Birthday' to Trevor. Bart and Bethany and I tried to talk him into it, but he just isn't comfortable with it, Mrs. Ryan. No offense to you, Trevor." Then Seal turned to me and said, "It's okay, Harv. I'll do it as soon as everyone has their cupcakes."

"Thanks. Thanks a lot," I said weakly.

Trevor gave me a funny look as he and Mom carted the baked goods to another group of kids.

Bart said, "After 'Happy Birthday,' how about leading us in singing, 'Rob and Leslie sitting in a tree, K-I-S-S-I-N-G. First comes love, then comes marriage, then comes *Harvey* in a baby carriage.'"

I felt sick to my stomach. Six hours too late.

ELEVEN

HIT THE ROAD, ROB

The bus ride back to school seemed even longer than the one to Auburn. Bart had shared his predictions for the future with everybody before we boarded the bus. Nobody pointed at them, but almost everybody whispered or giggled and sneaked looks in Mom and Mr. Stevens's direction. And in mine. I wouldn't have been surprised if Bethany had come right out and asked the couple about their future plans while we were bumping around the curves of Route 90.

The bus was quieter than in the morning. There's something about a bus bouncing through the countryside after lunch on a warm spring day that is tiring. I rolled up my jacket to use as a pillow and pretended to be napping so I wouldn't have to talk to anyone.

It wasn't long before I found myself floating over a baseball diamond. Mr. Stevens, in a Yankees uniform, rounded the bases to home plate, and the crowd cheered. "Batter up!" someone yelled, and Mom came out of the dugout wearing a wedding gown. Our minister, dressed like an umpire, stood behind home plate. Then I looked closer, and the minister was Bart! Bethany stood by Mom and held a baseball mitt in front of her. "What are your future plans, Mrs. Ryan? Or should I call you Mrs. Stevens?" she asked. With my dream eyes I zoomed in on the mitt and saw two wedding rings cradled in the palm of it. Trevor hawked baseball-shaped cupcakes and wedding pictures with stats written on the back, while the rest of my class looked out the windows of a school bus parked in front of the stands, whispering, giggling, and pointing. Where was I, I wondered? Then I saw Seal crossing over a bridge from Harriet Tubman's house to the ball field. She was dressed like a nurse and had a bundle in her arms. I zoomed in on the bundle and saw a baby wearing a uniform that said "Bat Boy—Harvey" on it. As she handed me to Mom and Mr. Stevens, I started to cry. Dad snapped pictures. I was blinded by the camera flash. I shook my head from side to side and woke up, realizing that it was the sun, not a camera, glaring in my eyes.

"You were whimpering like a baby," Seal said. "Were you dreaming?"

"No, I was having a nightmare. Promise me you'll never be a nurse."

"No problem." Seal shuddered. "You know I can't stand needles."

When we arrived back at school, it was time for activity period. It was a chorus day, so all the fifth-grade chorus members, including Seal, dumped their jackets and lunch leftovers on their desks and headed for the music room. Those left in the classroom worked on unfinished assignments or read. Mrs. Perkins reminded us that this would be a great opportunity to work on our writing-contest entries. I'd been putting mine off. I love to write, but the fact that Mom was involved made this taste bad, like when you think you have a glass of milk, take a big swig, and discover it's lemonade. I pulled out some fresh paper and wrote down some of the things that frustrate me about Mom.

After chorus Seal came over to my desk and said, "People were asking me about your mom and Mr. Stevens. They figured I would know the truth."

"Did you tell them it's none of their business?" I banged my fist on my desk.

"Of course not. That would only make them want to find out even more. I told them that as far as I knew they were just friends, but it wouldn't bother you a bit if they decided to date."

"Great. Now you're a liar too."

"Not exactly." Seal used her chorus music to fan herself. "That was all true a few weeks ago."

"It isn't true now!" I said between clenched teeth. "I'm sorry we started this whole thing. I'm even having nightmares in the middle of the day."

"There isn't much we can do about it now." Seal shrugged.

"We have to. We have to undo it." I noticed Bethany

edging closer to us, so I busied myself stuffing papers in my backpack. Seal scooted to her seat, and Mrs. Perkins asked for everyone's attention for some end-of-the-day announcements.

After the dismissal bell rang, we hurried out the door and bumped into Mom in the hallway.

"What are you still doing here?" I asked crossly.

Mom gave me that you're-being-rude-but-I-don't-want-to-holler-at-you-in-front-of-your-friends look and said, "I had some things I needed to discuss with Rob . . . Mr. Stevens. I thought you might like a ride home. Come along, Seal, you're on our way."

So Seal and I followed her to the car, keeping a safe distance between her and us. The fewer people who saw us together, the better.

After we dropped Seal off, Mom said, "I need to run into the store to pick up some hot dogs and buns. When Rob finishes in the office, he's coming by to grill them for us."

"Haven't you seen enough of each other today?" I asked rudely.

I knew I was very close to crossing the line, but Mom answered calmly. "I enjoy his company. Does that bother you?"

"No," I lied, wishing I could just blurt out, Yes!

"You see Seal in school and often again in the evening. I don't ask if you haven't seen enough of each other."

I was insulted. "She's my best friend!"

"And Rob is my new friend. You'll like him too, if you give him half a chance." Mom parked in front of Main Street Market. "Coming in? You can pick out some chips and soda to have with the dogs."

"Mom, what was Dad wearing when you got married?"

She looked at me strangely. "A tux. You've seen the pictures."

"That's right. Just making sure." I followed Mom into the store.

Back home after our shopping trip Mom told me to drag the grill out of the garage and dust it off. She also handed me a soapy rag to wash off the picnic table and benches. Then I threw balls at my pitching net, hard, while I waited for Mr. Stevens and supper.

Mr. Stevens arrived with Muddy Sneakers ice cream, unfortunately my favorite kind, and grilled the hot dogs to perfection. Mom had made baked beans and spinach salad. I had my first picnic of the season—my first two picnics actually, if you count sitting in the grass in Auburn—with my principal. We talked about the trip, and he asked me lots of baseball questions. For some reason I didn't feel much like talking baseball.

As soon as we finished eating, I asked if I could go to Seal's and show her my new stamps. They *had* arrived that day, and they *had* fit in the mailbox.

"I'd like to see your collection sometime," Mr. Stevens said.

Not in this lifetime, I thought as I hopped on my bike, but I yelled, "Sure. Some day soon," as I sped off.

I took the stamps with me, but Seal and I had more important business to take care of. Seal sat at her desk, notebook in hand, the way she had the day we dreamed up our first cockamamy scheme. I sat on her bed and bounced a ball off her footboard.

"This better work," I said, "because if it doesn't, I'm moving in with Dad."

"You have no faith in yourself."

"Well, do you have any ideas?"

"Not yet," she answered while she sharpened a pencil. "But we will. I'll make a list of ways to get rid of people."

I guess I was making more noise than I realized. Pete hollered from the living room, "You wanna knock off the racket in there?"

"Sure thing," I answered and carefully set the ball back on the floor.

"What if, after we get rid of him, Mr. Stevens takes it out on me?" I asked, continuing my conversation with Seal. "What if he makes me repeat fifth grade?"

"Principals can't do that. You'd have to fail to repeat. You're far from failing."

"I guess. But he could make my last year in the intermediate school very difficult."

"More difficult than this year? I think Mr. Stevens is too nice to do that."

"I guess. Let's get on with it." I tried not to think

about what a nice guy Mr. Stevens was. "This would be a lot easier if he were the kind of principal Mom used to have."

"If he were the kind of principal our parents had, none of this would be happening." Seal wrote, "Ways to Get Rid of People," at the top of a page in her notebook.

"In the old movie *The Leftovers*, some kids tried to get rid of some people by putting fleas inside their clothes. That would bug them!" I laughed at my own joke.

Seal laughed too. "It would be hard to do that. You'd have to be really close to him, and he'd wonder what you were doing."

"It would be easier to put bugs in his food."

Seal started to scratch at her neck. "That is so gross."

"But it's perfect! I could put a dead fly or spider or something on his plate when he's not looking. If it happened a few times, he'd think Mom is a terrible cook."

Seal wrote "Bug him!" in her notebook. "I think that you should only do something like that if our other ideas don't work first."

"What other ideas?" I asked, trying to ignore the tickly, itchy feeling in my pant legs.

"One of the ways to bug people—*annoy* them, Harvey—is to hang around them all the time. Just be in the way. Like the night Mr. Stevens was at your house eating apple cake. No man wants his girlfriend's kid underfoot every second. *Believe* me." Seal nodded her head toward the living room.

"So you want me to stick right to him."

"Like a wrapper on year-old Halloween candy." Seal wrote, "Stick it to him!" in her notebook. "What else is annoying?" she asked.

"It always bugs me when Mom writes things in her notebook when we're together. I wonder what she's writing and if it's about me. It makes me feel like I'm taking my clothes off in front of people."

"Two can play that game, Harvey!"

"Huh?"

"You can make them feel as uncomfortable as you do."

"This doesn't have anything to do with taking my clothes off, does it?" I could feel my eyes growing larger by the second.

Seal threw her pencil at me, and I ducked quickly, hoping it didn't clatter too loudly when it hit the wall.

"It has to do with writing," Seal said. "*You* can write things down too. In front of them and all the time. It will make them wonder what you're up to."

I picked up the pencil from behind the bed, brushed the dust bunny off it, and handed it to Seal. She wrote, "Keep them guessing" in the notebook.

I looked at my watch. "Yikes. It'll be dark soon. I better hit the road."

"Mr. Stevens better hit the road, too. Or he won't know what hit him."

"That's it!" I said.

"What's it?"

"The name of our new operation. Hit the road, Rob!"

Seal gave me a high five and wrote, "Hit the Road, Rob!" in her notebook. "That works."

"Let's hope it does."

TWELVE

KILL HIM WITH KINDNESS

Mr. Stevens was still there. As I pedaled past his Blazer, I had the horrifying urge to scrape my bike along the side of it. How could I even *think* such a thing? Just the thought made my legs start to wobble. I steadied myself and steered around the Blazer carefully. Get a grip, Harvey old boy. I took a deep breath, pasted on a smile, and hunted them down.

I heard laughter coming from the kitchen. I looked there first.

Mr. Stevens had a dish towel draped over his shoulder. If I didn't get rid of this guy soon, he'd be helping Mom hoe out the fridge!

"I'm glad you're still here, Mr. Stevens. Would you like to see my stamp collection now?"

"I'd love to, but I'm leaving in a few minutes. My poor cat has been alone all day."

"You have a *cat*? I *love* cats. I wish *I* had a cat, but poor Mom is *so* allergic to them, aren't you, Mom?"

"I used to think I was. Maybe I've outgrown it. That can happen, can't it?" Mom looked as if she hoped it could.

"You and Harvey can come to my place and meet Linus, and we'll see how you do. Harvey, I'll take a rain check on looking at that collection."

"Sure. How about tomorrow night?"

Mr. Stevens laughed. "I have a board meeting tomorrow night. But next time your mom invites me over, it's a deal."

I hung out until Mr. Stevens left. In fact, I walked out on the porch with him and Mom, and we stood there together and waved good-bye. I felt like Grandma and Grandpa Harvey, the way they see Mom and me off after a visit.

Mom ruffled my hair. "Thanks for being so nice to Rob. You really are a great kid."

Oh, brother. "You like him a lot, don't you?"

"I do. We seem to have so much in common. It's nice to be with someone like that."

I couldn't help thinking of Seal. How would I feel if someone tried to ruin our friendship? I *had* to stick with "Hit the Road, Rob," because I couldn't lie forever. But I didn't have to feel good about it.

The next morning I carried a notebook to the table.

"Did you forget about some homework?" Mom asked. She was pouring coffee into her oversized mug.

"No. You just never can tell when something interesting

is going to happen. I want to be ready in case I have to take notes." I spread peanut butter on a slice of warm toast.

"I see. So it's like a journal, then?"

"Not really." I sliced banana on top of the peanut butter toast.

"Oh, I see." Mom started to sit down with her coffee just as the dryer buzzed. The sudden noise startled her, some coffee slopped over the sides of the mug, and she squealed. I opened my notebook and recorded the event. Mom scowled at me.

When I put my plate in the dishwasher, I noticed a dead fly on the windowsill. When Mom wasn't looking, I dropped it into a zipper-top plastic bag and stuffed it in my pocket. It wouldn't hurt to be prepared.

I told Seal how well things were going. I also told her how crummy I'd felt out on the porch with Mom.

But having a plan to get rid of Mr. Stevens made it easier to face Bart at recess. When he started his "Rob and Leslie sitting in a tree" chant, I looked him straight in the eye and said, "Are you jealous or something?"

"Jealous? Of course not!"

"I think you are," said Seal. "It's a well-known fact that people try to pick on someone when they are jealous of them."

"And I think you're full of baloney," Bart snapped.

"I think Seal is right," said Bethany. "I would personally love to have a well-known mom dating someone important like Mr. Stevens."

"Are we going to play baseball or listen to a bunch of silly girls?" Bart demanded.

"I thought you'd never ask," I replied. "No offense, girls."

"None taken," said Seal.

Mr. Stevens didn't visit that night. But I bet that's who called as I was crawling into bed. I didn't lie awake and worry about it. I'd taken notes while Mom and I ate supper—she went to her office soon afterward—and I'd bagged another dead fly and the shriveled-up remains of a worm.

Bart didn't come outside for recess on Thursday. He told everyone he was working on the humorous-character writing assignment, but I bet he was in trouble and had to stay in. Without him pitching, it's a crime how easy it was to beat his team. I almost felt bad about how easy it was. *Almost.*

When Mom said Mr. Stevens would be coming over after supper, I said, "Great!" Then I carted my entire stamp collection into the dining room and spread it all over the table.

"There's a lot of stuff there. Don't you think you want to save some of it for another time?" Mom asked.

"I don't think so. Before long I'll be too busy with baseball season." And before long Mr. Stevens won't be around to see it, I thought.

Mom was a good sport about sharing Mr. Stevens with me for about an hour, but I noticed her looking at her watch several times. At seven-thirty she said, "Harvey, isn't it time for the Yankees game on TV?"

Mom wasn't playing fair. She usually tried to discourage me from watching TV, and she never suggested that I watch baseball even on a weekend, never mind a school night.

"I can catch a game another time. They play almost every day. Now *this*," I said to Mr. Stevens, "is the first commemorative stamp collection album my grandparents gave me. It came complete with stamps that were all issued that year and tells the story of each of them. They've given me one of these yearbooks every Christmas since I started collecting."

"Interesting," Mr. Stevens said, flipping through the pages. "This is a book of mini history lessons." He read the page about the space exploration stamps. "If I collected stamps, this would be the way I'd want to do it."

Not long after that, at least it didn't seem long to me, Mom said, "Don't you have some homework to do?"

"I did it after school," I said without looking up at her.

"I know you need to work on your writing contest entry. Best to do it tonight so you won't have it hanging over your head all weekend." Mom started to stack my books in a pile.

"All right. I'll show you the rest of my stamps tomorrow night, Mr. Stevens."

"Actually, I thought you and your mom could come to my place and meet Linus tomorrow evening. Is that okay, Leslie?"

"We'd be delighted," Mom said.

"Yes, delighted," I echoed.

I called Seal immediately. "I could have watched some of the Yankees game before working on this stupid contest, but no, I spent almost two hours with Mr. Stevens." I couldn't admit to Seal how much I'd enjoyed showing him my stamps. No one, other than Seal, had ever been so interested in them before.

"Maybe he'll disapprove of your mom suggesting you watch TV on a school night and decide he doesn't want her for a girlfriend after all," Seal said.

"That would make it too easy. After she told me about the game, he invited us over to his place tomorrow night. What kind of principal is he?"

After school on Friday Seal and I looked up Mr. Stevens's address in the phone book. It was only a few blocks away, so we decided to take a bike ride to his neighborhood to check out his house before Mom and I went there.

I knew it was his place even before I saw the house number because of the black Blazer parked in the driveway. The house was old brick with a historical date plaque by the front door. I couldn't read the date because we were across the street.

While we watched from beside a bush loaded with little yellow flowers, a minivan pulled into Mr. Stevens's driveway. A woman about Mom's age stepped out of it, and Mr. Stevens ran out of the house and gave the woman a big hug and kiss.

Seal gasped. "I don't think we were supposed to see that!"

"Let's get *out* of here." I was already on my bike, heading toward home.

"That two-timer. So much for nice Mr. Stevens," said Seal after we rounded the corner.

"What kind of principal is he?" I found myself asking for the second time in two days. "I was really starting to like him, too," I admitted, "and now I find out he's nothing but a dirty rat! What am I going to tell my mom?"

"I don't know, but I don't think it would be a good idea for you to go over to his house tonight."

"Do you think that lady would still be there? Poor Mom. She's been so happy lately."

"Look, you wanted to get rid of Mr. Stevens, didn't you? He's just made your job a lot easier. We can forget 'Hit the Road, Rob,'" said Seal.

"But what a waste of good bugs. And poor Mom," I said again. "What will she do?"

"She'll get over it," Seal said as my house came into sight. "She still has her writing."

"Don't remind me!"

Seal didn't come in the house with me. She decided Pete and her mom expected her home. She'd turned into a liar too.

I opened the front door and saw Mom sitting on the stairs changing from sneakers to good shoes. She had on a jean jumper and her hair was pulled back in a clip. She looked young and pretty. My heart ached for her because of what I had to tell her. "Mom—"

"There you are, Harvey. It's almost time to go to Rob's. He called this morning and said his sister decided to visit for the weekend while her children are on a Boy Scout camping trip with their dad. He expected her to arrive this afternoon, and he wants us to come over and have pizza with them." Mom made a face, wrinkling up her nose. "Why don't you put on a clean shirt?"

I pulled at the front of my T-shirt, unsticking it from my sweaty chest. "His sister, you said? Mr. Stevens has a sister?" I could tell that my voice was squeaking.

"Yes, but don't be nervous. I'm nervous already. If you're nervous too, I'll fall apart!" Mom smoothed the front of her jumper.

"Well, don't be," I said, trying to steady my voice. "She looks nice."

"What?"

"I mean, she *sounds* nice. I mean, she *must* be nice if Mr. Stevens is her brother." I smiled weakly.

"Harvey, that's a *nice* thing to say." Mom stood up

and kissed my cheek. "Now run upstairs and change that shirt. You're drenched. You look as if you biked straight uphill."

"I guess I was in a hurry. Didn't want to be late for Mr. Stevens." Unfortunately, I muttered to myself as I climbed the stairs, he's not a bad guy after all.

THIRTEEN

I HATE IT WHEN . . .

I hate to say that we had a good time at Mr. Stevens's house, so I'll just say it was okay.

Linus looked like a giant orange puffball and was a really cool cat. Mr. Stevens named him Linus because he's always had a special blanket he likes to sleep on. Mr. Stevens said that whenever he puts it in the washer, Linus paces around the house waiting until it's back again. Linus likes cheese off pizza, too. He helped me eat mine and then curled up on my lap while we sat in the living room, even without his blanket. Mom's eyes didn't water at all, and she didn't sneeze once.

Terry, that's Mr. Stevens's sister, *is* nice. After we were introduced, I realized she was the woman in the picture in Mr. Stevens's office. The kids in the picture must have been her boys. Maybe the old people were her and Mr. Stevens's parents.

Terry and Mom had a lot to talk about. Terry is a teacher and has read Mom's books to her students and her two boys, who are a little younger than me. She said I'd have to meet her boys during summer vacation. She was sure they'd be disappointed not to have met Mom and me that weekend. I knew that would change by summertime.

Mr. Stevens offered to show me around the house while the ladies talked and said he was sure he could find a deck of cards or something for me to play with. But I didn't want to disturb Linus or get too far away from the conversation. So Mr. Stevens handed me the remote control to the TV. Linus and I clicked through the channels several times before settling on the Cartoon Network. I cheered when the cat trapped the mouse under a teacup, and Linus purred.

On the way home Mom explained that Mr. Stevens had been married many years ago, but that his wife had died when a drunk driver hit her car head-on. Wow. I really didn't need to hear anything that made me feel sorry for him. I was trying not to like him, but except for his being a principal, I couldn't find much wrong with him.

I guess Mom thought I was too quiet. "Do you feel all right?" she asked. "If you become ill at your dad's, I'm worried he won't know what to do for you."

"I feel fine," I said sharply. I hate it when she says things that make Dad sound irresponsible. I hate it even more when he does something that proves her right.

Of course I didn't get sick, but right after Dad picked me up Saturday morning, he said he and Mindy had an important meeting to go to and I'd have to amuse myself for a while.

I amused myself by working on the writing project for the contest. I'd scribbled some notes, but so far I hadn't settled on an interesting character. Then I looked over the notes I'd written during the week about Mom. And it hit me, just like a baseball dropping neatly into my glove, who my character would be.

By the time Dad returned, I had my contest entry done and was roller-blading in the tavern parking lot.

"We have great news, Harvey. But how would you like to grab some lunch and play a round of mini golf first?"

"Jake, you shouldn't tease him," Mindy said. She was smiling too.

Dad pretended to be offended. "I'm not teasing him! I just thought this would be a great way to tell him the news."

"What is it?" I asked.

"Do you want to play mini golf or not?" Dad asked.

"Of course I do." I was hurrying to remove my roller blades.

We went to a course on the lake. Every hole represented something important to New York State, like the Statue of Liberty, a longhouse, or a dairy farm. I caught myself thinking that Mr. Stevens would like this place.

The Finger Lakes were laid out in miniature at the ninth hole, and it was tricky to hit the golf ball past them without having it drop in the little pockets of water. If you could hit the ball across Niagara Falls at the eighteenth hole, you won a free game. Of course Dad made it across, but we didn't have time to play the free game because he and Mindy needed to be at the tavern.

"Do you think you'd like to come here again?" Dad asked after we'd returned our clubs to the teenager working behind the counter.

"I'd love to! And I want to bring Seal sometime."

"Then here's that great news I was saving for after our game." Dad glanced over at Mindy and smiled. "That meeting we had this morning was with the owner of this place. He wants to sell. And Mindy and I are buying it. Think you'd like to work here during the summer? You could play all the mini golf you want, too."

I started jumping up and down like a little kid. "That's the best news I've had since you told me you'd coach my baseball team!"

Dad and Mindy looked at each other. When Mindy looked at me, I thought she might start to cry.

"What is it?" I asked. "What did I say?"

"I'm not sure how to tell you, son, but with me taking on another business this summer, I'm not going to be able to coach your team."

"What? What? You promised!"

"Now, Harvey, I never actually promised. I said I'd like to. And I *would* like to. But not this year."

"Not *this* year!" I shouted. "Not *any* year!" And I knew if I didn't walk away, I would start crying like a little kid. Out of the corner of my eye I saw Mindy put her hand on Dad's arm to keep him from following me. They joined me in the car a few minutes later.

"I'm sorry I let you down," Dad said into the rearview mirror. "I'm sure you'll find a good coach, and I know you'll have a great team."

"Of course you're disappointed now, Harvey. I am too." Mindy twisted around in the front seat so she could look at me. "But in the long run I think you'll be happy that we're buying the golf course. You'll always have a summer job. Maybe someday you'll even want to run it yourself."

"Maybe. When I'm too old to play baseball. Too bad I'm not planning to play professional golf."

We were quiet for the rest of the ride back to the house.

Dad and Mindy's house is attached to the back side of the tavern, so it works out well when I spend the night. Before the busy time I go in the tavern and fill the snack dishes with peanuts and light the candles on the tables. In warmer weather my favorite tables are the ones on the porch because the view of the lake is great and I love the smell of the boat fuel and the citronella candles that help keep mosquitoes away. I know all the people who work there, but my favorite is Benny. He calls me Boss. During the rest of the evening Dad and Mindy come in and out of the house to check on me and bring me sodas and chips. Sometimes one of them watches TV with me.

Dad brought me a buddy burger and watched several innings of a Yankees game with me that night. And Mindy brought me a huge helping of peanut butter pie with extra whipped cream. I wasn't ready to forgive Dad yet, even though I knew I'd love hanging out at the golf course.

I wondered why every time something good happened to me, it had to have some bad mixed with it. Dad being a baseball player couldn't just be a good thing. It had to take him away from us. Mom being a writer couldn't just be a good thing because she had to write about me. Even Mom finding a nice man made my life difficult. And now Dad couldn't coach my team because of a wonderful, crummy golf course.

Before Dad took me home on Sunday, we played a little ball. Dad said my form looked good, and I was pitching faster than last year. There's a lot of energy in anger.

FOURTEEN

LOVE IS ALL AROUND

When Dad, Mindy, and I walked into the house that Sunday, I guess I didn't look too good. I was still feeling pretty sad. I guess Mom thought I looked sick. She turned to Dad, eyes flashing.

"Why didn't you call me? I would have picked him up last night."

"I'm not sick! Can't a kid ever not feel totally happy with his life for a minute without you thinking he's sick or making a big deal out of it?"

"What is going on?" Mom demanded.

"I'll explain," Dad said, and then told her how he'd let me down.

"I knew this would happen. Are you completely incapable of following through on anything?" Mom asked.

"Now wait," Dad said. "I'm running a very successful business."

"Jake's a great father," said Mindy. "He's wonderful with Harvey. He wishes he *could* coach this summer."

"Listen," I said, quick to defend Dad when someone else was mad at him, "it's not the end of the world. I'll get over it, all right?"

"You're a good boy," said Mindy.

"We'll see you in two weeks, Buddy," Dad said as he grabbed my shoulders. "You're going to love the golf course."

"Already do," I mumbled. "See you."

And they left.

Mom hugged me and said how sorry she was that things hadn't worked out.

"It's not the first time. It won't be the last," I said, trying not to cry in front of her.

"Welcome to the world of Jake Ryan."

That bothered me. I know Dad's not perfect, but who is? Besides, I'd been in Jake Ryan's world my whole life, and most of it *had* been pretty good.

Mom pasted a smile on her face. "Rob is coming over tonight after Terry leaves. I bet he'd love to finish looking through your stamps."

"Maybe. I'd like to find out what Seal is doing." She was the only person I cared about who never let me down. I went upstairs to use the phone.

Seal wasn't home, I learned in the world's shortest conversation with Pete, so I went to my room and oiled my baseball glove. I knew Dad was a good man and that he loved me. Somehow, when Mom got mad at him, I felt less angry at him myself. Less angry and a little sadder. A couple of tears dropped down onto my glove, and I rubbed them, along with the oil, into the soft leather.

I heard Mr. Stevens arrive, but I didn't go downstairs. Instead I listened at my half-opened door.

"You are wonderful," he was saying to Mom. "Terry thinks you're terrific, too. These last few weeks have made me happier than I ever thought I could be."

Mom laughed and said something too softly for me to hear. In the quiet space that followed, I guessed they must be kissing.

I pushed my door closed, feeling like an intruder in my own home. Then I pulled the plastic bag out of my pocket and dropped it in my wastebasket. Things had gone too far and I was admitting defeat. Mr. Stevens was not going to be chased off by a bothersome boy or a bag full of bugs. Mr. Stevens was in love. And it was all my fault.

"Harvey, come downstairs," Mom called. "Rob wondered if we'd like to go to the movies."

On a Sunday night? Mom must have told him about Dad, and they were trying to make me feel better. I wasn't going to argue. I met them at the bottom of the stairs.

"Would you like to take your friend Seal with us?" Mr. Stevens asked. "That is, if she's allowed to go on a school night."

"I'll see if she's home yet. She's allowed, believe me," I said.

Seal answered the phone on the first ring, saving me from talking to good old Pete again. I gave her the condensed version of the weekend and told her we'd pick her up in twenty minutes. "Of course, knowing my luck, Bart will be there and he'll think we're on a double date," I concluded.

"I can handle it, Harvey."

"I know you can. That's what I love about you. I mean—"

"I know what you mean. See you later."

To my relief, the Bartholomews' Sunday-evening plans did not include the movies.

"I think we should sit in the first row," Mom said while we were standing in line to buy popcorn.

"No way. They're terrible seats," I complained.

"I'm just kidding," Mom said. And she and Mr. Stevens laughed for about five minutes.

"Cute couple," Seal whispered in my ear.

"I know," I said. Ain't fate funny?

FIFTEEN

PROBLEMS, PROBLEMS, PROBLEMS

We turned in our contest entries the next day. The fifth-grade teachers planned to read through them and select the top five or so from each class, then pass them on to Mom for a final decision. A lot had happened in the past two days. If I'd had time to change my character, I would have. But like so many things I'd done lately, I couldn't undo it now. Maybe I'd be lucky for a change, and my essay wouldn't pass the teachers' cut.

Things were so busy in school I didn't have much time to think about all my problems. With Young Authors' Day a week away, the entire school was rushing to finish all the projects that would be on display. My pieces on Harriet Tubman and stamp collecting were going in. We spent recess every day illustrating our entries and binding them into booklets. That meant there was no time to play baseball.

We stopped playing baseball in gym that week too, because the gym teachers decided to work in a unit of lacrosse. In some ways that was a relief, but I was worried about not practicing enough before summer league started. I was sure Dad had called the guy in charge of the recreation department and told him he wouldn't be coaching, but I hadn't worked up the nerve to tell the guys yet. Wouldn't *that* make Bart's summer!

Bart and I weren't exactly on speaking terms, but he snarled in my direction every now and then. It's a good thing he didn't know how much he bothered me, or I'm sure he'd have been even worse. The day we turned in our writing contest assignments, he said to his friends, loudly enough for me to hear, "It doesn't matter what any of us wrote. Harvey will win with his mom judging the stupid thing. Especially now that she's dating the principal."

"I think Harvey *should* win. He's cute. And I bet he writes good, too." Bethany smiled in my direction. She is the major reason why I'll never have a girlfriend.

Seal came over Friday evening to watch a movie with me while Mom and Mr. Stevens went out for supper. The high school kid from next door came too, but he had to finish track practice and shower first, so he wasn't there yet when Mom left.

Mom was still talking to me as they went out the door. "Chris will be here in less than an hour, Harvey. And his dad can be here in half a minute if you need anything. And don't eat the snacks first. There are fresh rolls for subs. I'll have the cell phone with me, and the number is on the speed dialer if you need anything. We'll be home by—"

"I know, I know," I interrupted. "You'll be home by eight o'clock at the latest. And you're only two blocks away. Just go already. We'll be fine." I pushed the door closed behind them, hoping it wouldn't take them too long to get in the Blazer and out of plain sight.

Seal and I shook our heads at each other.

"They act like we're a couple of kindergarten babies," I said.

"So what do you have good to eat?" she asked.

We popped corn, filled two tumblers with orange juice, then flopped down on the couch with our snack supper. I put on the movie, and we talked through the previews.

"The fifth-grade teachers finished choosing the best new character essays from each class. Mr. Stevens brought them to our doorstep right after school." I crammed a handful of popcorn in my mouth.

"Has your mom looked through them yet?" Seal nibbled at her popcorn one kernel at a time.

I shook my head while I swallowed. "No, that's her big weekend project. She told Mr. Stevens and me that she would need some time to herself to read them and decide on the winning character."

Seal sat up straighter. "Aren't you dying to know whose he brought over?"

"I hadn't thought about it." Now I was even lying to

Seal. I pawed through the popcorn looking for burned kernels, which are my favorite.

"Are they in her study? We could go look." Seal took the bowl out of my hands and set it on the coffee table.

"There aren't any names on them, remember?" I leaned forward, trying to reach the popcorn. "Just numbers, so the judging would be fair."

"True, but don't you at least want to know if yours is in there? Or mine? We'd recognize our own." Seal tugged at my arm, trying to make me stand up.

"I guess it wouldn't hurt to check." We put the movie on pause, freezing a superhero in the middle of the screen.

I'll never be able to make a living as a thief. Just the thought of going into Mom's study without being invited made my hands sweat. Seal and I didn't turn the hall light on, and we didn't say a word as we tiptoed into the hall and up the stairs, feeling our way along the banister and then the smooth papered wall.

When we reached Mom's door, lights from a car heading toward our house flooded through the front windows. Seal and I froze, my hand stuck to the doorknob.

"This is ridiculous," Seal whispered after the car drove by. "They won't be home for at least an hour. Their dinners probably haven't been served yet."

"You're right." I laughed nervously. "We don't need to act like a couple burglars! This is my own house! We aren't going to *steal* anything. We're just checking to see if something that belongs to us is *here*."

"Now you're talking, partner." Seal slugged me.

"Take it easy on the pitching arm," I said, unsticking my hand to massage my right biceps.

Seal opened the door. I clicked on the desk lamp, sending a circle of light on the desk like beams from a flying saucer hovering over a field.

The essays were there, in a pile by Mom's computer. I reached for them, then hesitated.

"What if she notices that we've moved them?" I asked.

"We aren't planning to leave them in another room. They'll be right here where she left them. Besides, now that she's in love, you'll be able to get away with a lot without her noticing."

I groaned and handed half the stack to Seal. I began pawing through the other half.

Seal laughed. "This one is a riot. I wonder whose it is."

"We don't have time to *read* them!" I snapped.

"All *right*. You don't have to be so panicky." Seal sat down in Mom's swivel chair and propped her feet up on the desk. "Here's mine! Want to read it?"

"NO."

Seal continued to flip through the essays. "Here's one with a drawing attached. It's of a *princess*. It *has* to be Bethany's."

I groaned at the mention of her name.

"I've sifted through this whole pile, and my essay isn't in it, Seal. See if you have it."

"Isn't this your handwriting?" She held up a paper she'd separated from the rest.

I stared at it and nodded. I waved Seal off Mom's chair and sat down.

"What's the matter?" she asked. "I thought you were in a hurry to get out of here."

"I have to read this first," I said, taking my paper from Seal. "I thought this was funny when I wrote it, and I thought it would be a way to show Mom how I feel when she writes about me. Now I'm afraid it will make her mad. I think I'll just pull it out of the pile and keep it in my journal, like the thank-you note I wrote when Mom visited our class."

"You can't do that. Mrs. Perkins would know it's missing when your mom sends them back to school."

"I'd rather have Mrs. Perkins mad at me than Mom. Maybe I'll move in with Dad. I can wash golf balls and fill peanut dishes for the rest of my life. No more Bart. No more embarrassing mother. No more Mr. Stevens."

"And no more summer baseball and no more Seal," Seal reminded me.

"They play summer ball everywhere. And you can come visit."

Seal put her hands on her hips and shook her head sadly. "You can't run away from your problems, Harvey."

"Why not? I can't *fix* them."

"You can learn to make the best of what you have."

"I'd rather run away."

SIXTEEN

SECRETS

Sleeping shouldn't be a big problem for a healthy, growing boy like me, right? That should be as easy as eating ice cream on a hot summer day. But one thing or another kept standing between me and a good night's rest.

Mom was busy in her study, probably reading essays, when I dragged myself out of bed Saturday morning. I fixed strawberry shortcake for my breakfast, deciding I might as well enjoy one thing about the day.

I wondered how long it would take Mom to read a couple dozen essays. When lunchtime was near, I tiptoed to the study door and listened for signs of life. I don't know if their scalp tingles or their palms sweat or just what happens, but moms know when their kids are nearby, even if they can't see or hear them. Maybe it's an odor we put out that only mothers can smell. Whatever it is, Mom knew I was only a few feet away.

"Come in, Harvey."

"I don't want to bother you. I just wondered if you would like some lunch," I called.

Mom opened the door and motioned me toward her. "Let's chat first."

I had no choice but to go into her study.

Mom sat down in her swivel desk chair and folded her arms in front of her. Since hers was the only chair in the room, I stood by her desk. It felt like I'd been held after school for a meeting with a teacher.

"It's rather obvious which essay you wrote," she began.

"Did you recognize my handwriting?" I started to fidget with the pencil holder on the desk.

"That, and the fact that not too many other kids would create a character who spies on her classmates and family members, then writes about them and embarrasses everyone. Funny stuff, Harvey."

But Mom wasn't smiling. I laughed nervously, and tipped over the container. Pens and pencils clattered onto the desk and floor. Mom ignored the interruption.

"It's interesting that her name is Leslie Lyon, but that the other kids call her Lyin' Leslie," she continued. "And that she convinces a friend of hers to take photos to go along with the stories she writes."

I was busy picking up writing utensils. And busy not looking at Mom.

Then she said in a softer and more motherly voice, "I know you were sending me a message with that character, Harvey. I heard you loud and clear. And I'm sorry."

I dared look at her. She had that dopey sad smile like when we were watching a TV show about puppies being rescued out of a drainpipe.

"Are you mad at me?" I asked, edging a little closer to the door.

"Of course not. But I *am* embarrassed. I'm sure Mrs. Perkins noticed that Lyin' Leslie is a caricature of me. Why didn't you tell me how you felt about the stories I write before this?"

"I don't know. I guess I thought that somebody who knows how to make other kids laugh should know what makes their own kid sad." I looked down at my feet and noticed that one of my shoelaces had come undone.

"Oh, Harvey, now I really feel awful."

Mom leaned forward in her seat as if her hearing had failed and she needed to get closer to hear me. "How does what I write make you sad?" she asked.

"It doesn't make me sad exactly. It embarrasses me." I couldn't take my eyes off that shoelace.

"How so?" she asked. "What I write is a little bit about you, but it's mostly made up."

"Mostly," I said as I brought my eyes level with Mom's. "But everyone knows that I had a crush on my second-grade teacher, and that I loaded our groceries into the backseat of the wrong car at the store, and that I clogged the kitchen sink with Cream of Wheat."

Mom smiled. "Those aren't bad things. They're funny."

"They're *private*," I said, desperately wanting her to understand.

Mom closed her eyes for a moment and nodded. "I see what you mean. I know I keep saying it, but I *am* sorry. Has all of it been awful for you?"

"No," I said, and realized that was true. "I *am* proud of you, but I'd like it better if you wrote about other things." I swallowed hard. "And I'm sorry I've made you feel embarrassed in front of Mrs. Perkins. I guess it would have been smarter to try to talk to you. But you seemed to know everything else about me. Maybe I thought you knew how I felt about the things you write but didn't care."

"I'll *always* care how you feel." Mom stood up and held me tight against her for a moment. "You are growing up on me. I wasn't going to be able to write about things you do much longer anyway. Are you hungry?" she asked.

I nodded, a little afraid I might start to cry with all this mushy talk about feelings.

Mom turned me around and nudged me toward the door. "Let's fix a sandwich and continue this discussion in the kitchen."

Mom and I made two huge corned beef on rye sandwiches and opened a jar of Grandma's homemade dill pickles and a bag of cookies, then sat down at the kitchen table.

"Harvey, I'll let you in on a little secret. When I was

in school I *did* write things about my classmates. One time I wrote something mean about some girls who weren't nice to me, and they found it. They took it to the principal, and I was in trouble."

"What did he do?" This was shocking news, and I wondered if she'd ever shared it with Mr. Stevens. I couldn't imagine Mom ever being in trouble.

"I spent recess for the rest of the week in his office. First I had to write apologies to the girls, and then I had to write a compliment about everyone in my class. That experience taught me an important lesson about writing unkind things. You taught me another lesson about other people's feelings today."

I wanted to hear more about what Mom had written that was awful enough for her to be sent to the principal's office, but I was working on swallowing a big bite of corned beef and couldn't ask with my mouth full.

"You are an excellent writer, Harvey. Your essay was a real winner. Do you understand why I can't choose it above all the others? It has nothing to do with the character embarrassing me."

"Everybody would think you chose it because I'm your son. Some of the kids already think I'm going to win for that reason. And because you're friends with Mr. Stevens."

Mom's sandwich stopped halfway to her mouth. "Have they been giving you a hard time about that?"

"A little." I shrugged my shoulders, trying to convince both of us that it wasn't a big deal.

I could tell Mom wasn't convinced and was working out the right thing to say. She probably wanted to ask who'd been bothering me.

"Do you really think my writing is good?" I asked.

"I think your writing is good enough for you to become a writer someday, if you want to."

"I like to write. I think I like it as much as playing baseball. Do you think I could be a writer *and* a baseball player?"

Some adults would have laughed at that, but Mom didn't. "It's possible," she said. "Some people can only do one thing well at a time. They focus so hard on that one goal that nothing else matters. I've been like that, but I'm trying to change. And if you're prepared for the challenge, I believe you could make it work." Mom took two cookies, then slid the package over to me.

"Are you trying to make more than one thing work? Are you trying to focus on more than just writing?"

"Yes, I am." Mom broke one of the cookies in half and quickly dunked a piece in her milk before popping it in her mouth.

I put a handful of cookies on my napkin. "Is Mr. Stevens your new focus?"

She nodded slowly. "He's part of it."

"Do you think you'll—*marry* him?" Now that I'd started to have an honest conversation with Mom, that question came out easier than I'd expected.

"I'm taking things one day at a time. I'm not going to

rush into another marriage. Rob understands that. But it could happen."

"If it does, would you mind waiting till I'm in junior high?"

Mom leaned across the table and kissed the top of my head. "I think we could handle that. Now I have to get back to work."

We picked up our dishes and carried them to the sink. "Mom," I said, "you're a good writer too."

"Thanks, sweetie. That means a lot coming from you."

I love how young Mom looks when she smiles.

Mom made her decision about the winning essay later that afternoon. Even though I knew she hadn't picked mine, it felt great to know she thought I was a good writer. I still wanted to play in the majors, but if that didn't work out, I'd rather write than own a golf course or a restaurant. Not that there is anything wrong with those things. I just have other plans.

Mr. Stevens showed up at our door with Chinese food at five. "I'm sorry," he said when Mom let him in. "I know I told you I'd leave you alone today, but you need to take a break for supper."

Mom laughed. "Your timing couldn't be better. I was about to call and let you know I finished with the essays."

The smell of soy sauce, sweet-and-sour pork, and steamed rice creeping from the bags in Mr. Stevens's hands made me hungry. "I'll set the table," I said. I took the paper sacks and headed for the kitchen. I looked back over my shoulders in time to see Mr. Stevens give Mom a quick kiss on the lips. It didn't look all that bad. But I was glad they'd closed the outside door. You never know when somebody could be watching your house from across the street.

During supper Mom said, "If you two boys can keep a secret, I'll tell you something about the winning character."

"Sure!" we said in unison.

"It's a baseball player. I'm finally going to write about a baseball player."

"That's great," I said. "You've written stories about almost everything I've ever done. How come you never wrote about a baseball player before?"

Mom plopped a spoonful of rice on her plate before answering. "Baseball is not exactly my favorite subject. But this character has such interesting possibilities it will be fun to work him into a story."

"Speaking of baseball," Mr. Stevens said, wiping the corners of his mouth with his napkin, "do you know if they've found a coach for your team, Harvey?"

"I don't think so. Do you know someone who would be interested?"

"I've been thinking about doing it myself."

I almost dropped my chopsticks. I heard Mom murmur, "Oh, Rob, how nice."

Then Mr. Stevens said, "I played a little ball in school."

"What college?" I asked, deciding this might turn out okay.

Mr. Stevens laughed. "Oh, not in college. Or high school even. Just a little summer-league ball when I was about your age."

"Oh," I said, trying to keep the disappointment out of my voice. "I'm sure the director would be happy to know you're interested. If they haven't found anybody else yet. Could I be excused?"

"You haven't eaten much, but go ahead if you're full," Mom said. "We'll save the fortune cookies for later."

"Thanks," I muttered. I bet my fortune would be a real winner. Not.

SEVENTEEN

AND THE WINNER IS . . .

I thought I was prepared for Mom's Young Authors' Day speech, but all I was prepared for was not winning the contest. I was not prepared to hear her say, "And the winner is . . . Brian Bartholomew!" I had no idea he could be humorous, let alone write. I didn't hear anything that Mom said after that because I was thinking about how Bart would have to spend time with Mom, probably at our house, now that his baseball player was her newest character.

Seal poked me in the ribs. "Look at Bart's face! He was so sure this contest was rigged that he can't believe his ears."

"It serves him right," I muttered.

"Don't be a poor sport."

"I'm *not* a poor sport. I'd be happy for anyone else on this planet if they won." I noticed Bethany twisted around in her seat, staring at me. "Well, *almost* anyone."

I was sure my summer was ruined, what with Bart

winning the contest and summer-league practices starting the following week.

I guess people weren't lining up to coach. Some kids
said we were lucky to at least have Mr. Stevens. I doubted
it. A lot of kids were surprised by how nice he was. But
nice doesn't win games if you don't know how to play
ball.

The turnaround came during our third baseball
game. Dad was there and had watched us lose our first
two games. Between the third and fourth inning of this
game, which we were already losing by four runs, Dad
went over to Mr. Stevens. I don't know what he said, but
Dad started to give some pointers to the guys before they
went up to bat, and Mr. Stevens changed some of the
playing positions in the bottom of the inning. The
things Dad suggested worked. The other team didn't
score again. We brought in five runs, just enough to finally win a game.

After the game, Dad and Mr. Stevens shook hands. I
walked toward them to say good-bye to Dad.

"Your dad has just agreed to be an informal assistant
coach," Mr. Stevens told me.

"Hooray!" I jumped up and down.

Seal, who came to all my games, touched my arm and
said under her breath, "Look at your mom." Mom was
standing apart from the group and didn't look as happy
as everyone else seemed to be. I wondered if she and Mr.
Stevens were going to have their first fight.

"I won't make every game, or many practices, but I'll be happy to help when I'm here," Dad said.

"And we'll be happy for that help anytime, won't we, Harvey?" said Mr. Stevens.

"We sure will!" I was embarrassed when everybody laughed. A smile even brightened Mom's face for a second.

Dad turned and caught sight of her. "Do you mind, Leslie?"

Mom shrugged. "If you're going to be here as much as you can anyway, you might as well help Harvey's team."

Dad loaded baseballs into the team bag. Mr. Stevens put his arm around Mom's shoulders. "Thank you," I heard him say softly. "It will be okay. I promise."

You have to like a guy like that.

The rest of the season, and summer, sped by. I spent about half the time between practice and game days at Dad's. Sometimes Seal went with me. We took our stamp collections with us, used the paddleboat, and fished, and Seal learned to water-ski. We played mini golf too. Lots of mini golf. I was on my way to being an unbeatable player.

I wish I could say the same for my baseball team. Bart's team came out ahead of mine by the end of the season, but I am proud to say that when our teams played each other, they didn't beat us even once. Dad made it to almost every game and a handful of practices, and just like Mr. Stevens had promised, it was okay.

Mom stopped acting mad at Dad all the time, and I think she learned to like Mindy a little. By the end of the season they were sitting together at my ball games! Mr. Stevens wasn't the best coach I'd ever had, but he did get better as the season wore on, and he did learn a lot about baseball.

Bart and I still aren't best friends and never will be. But now we can be in the same room without drawing a crowd of interested spectators. It was awkward the first time he came to our house to work on his baseball character with Mom. I think he was both proud and embarrassed. I was still trying to recover from the shock. He still rags on me a little about Mom and Mr. Stevens, but he hasn't poked fun at me about Mom's books since he started working with her.

When Mom isn't working on her baseball book, she and Mr. Stevens are working on a book about the Underground Railroad. They've already decided that when they finish this one, they're going to write one about the Erie Canal. I'm surrounded by history.

One evening toward the end of summer Mom sent me outside with a plate of cheese slices for Mr. Stevens to put on the burgers he was grilling.

"Those hamburgers smell great, Mr. Stevens. Mom bought that cheese you and I like on ours."

Mr. Stevens flipped the burgers and took the plate from my hands. "Harvey, we've spent a lot of time together this summer, and I want you to know I plan to stick around. I don't think it's a secret how I feel about your mom, or you."

I looked down at my feet and studied my shoelaces, hoping he wouldn't see the red blotches I could feel forming on my cheeks.

Mr. Stevens kept talking. "Every time you call me Mr. Stevens, I feel as if we're in school. It's much too formal for our new relationship. I wondered if you'd like to call me Rob."

I looked up at him. He patted the cheese in place with the spatula, then looked back at me, waiting for me to say something.

"I don't know," I said. "I mean, I'd *like* to, but we *will* be in school soon. What if I mess up and call you . . . and call you by your first name there."

"People wouldn't mind. They'd understand."

"But the kids might think you were treating me better than everyone else. They might think I felt like I was better than them or something."

"Umm. I see your point. That could be a problem." The cheese had melted and looked like a soft yellow skin on the hamburgers. Mr. Stevens used the spatula to lift them onto the platter.

"Uh-oh," I said. "I was supposed to give Mom a five-minute warning so she could bring out the rolls and salad and drinks."

"We'll help her. Give my problem some thought and let me know if you have any ideas, okay?"

"Sure thing, Mr. Stevens. Oops."

"Harv," he said, and waited for me to look up at him. "It's okay." Then he pointed toward the house with the spatula.

I'm in sixth grade now. I'm sure Mom will be invited in to talk, especially if her book with Bart's baseball character is published before school is out. Bart, Seal, and I are in the same room this year. (Bethany is not. I really need to thank whoever makes up the class lists.)

Seal and I have been talking about starting a school newspaper like the one they have in the high school. We've even thought about asking Bart to write a sports column. I guess I could live with that as long as I was the editor. Who'd ever have thought he'd be able to write! Just goes to show how little you really know about people. We've joked about asking Bethany to write a gossip column, but people's feelings might be hurt. And we want to send copies of the paper to our grandparents.

Everyone in school is getting used to Mom and Mr. Stevens being a couple. Even me. But I'll still be glad to move on to junior high next year, like every other sixth-grader I know. By then most of the kids will have outgrown Mom, even if teachers over there invite authors of local history in to speak to their classes. Like I said to Seal last night, "I'll have to make the best of it."

"Now where have I heard that before?" Seal set down

the tweezers she was using to separate stamps in order to give me her full attention.

I ignored her question, but I did say, "You know what I was thinking? Maybe we aren't the reason Mom and Mr. Stevens got together. Maybe that would have happened anyway. Maybe some things are just meant to be."

"Like fate," said Seal. "Maybe. But I think we helped a little. At least we sped things up. And you got your Mom to stop writing about you."

"True," I agreed. "But I don't think there's a whole lot we can do to change other people. All we can do is work on ourselves. You know, make our own lives be the best they can be."

"Does that mean you aren't going to try to manage other people's lives anymore?"

"Yeah. I've got enough of my own stuff to work on."

"Me too." Seal pulled the hair band off her ponytail and shook her long black hair loose. "How does Mr. Stevens like you calling him Coach?"

I grinned. "He loves it."